The Quickenii

The Quickening Pulse

Books 1–5

to accompany
Excellence in English Books 1–5

The Quickening Pulse

Book 1

Selected by D J Brindley

HODDER AND STOUGHTON
LONDON SYDNEY AUCKLAND TORONTO

I should like to thank my wife for her devoted help in the preparation of this manuscript.

1979   DJB

British Library Cataloguing in Publication Data

The quickening pulse.
  Book 1
  1. Short stories, English
  1. Brindley, David James
  823'.9'1 FS   PR1309.S5

ISBN 0 340 23493 8

First published 1979
Selection copyright © 1979 D J Brindley

Printed and bound in Great Britain for
Hodder and Stoughton Educational,
a division of Hodder and Stoughton Ltd,
Mill Road, Dunton Green, Sevenoaks, Kent,
by Hazell Watson & Viney Ltd, Aylesbury, Bucks

Contents

The Boy and the Badger *by E T Seton*

In 1871 there was a family named Service living at Bird's Hill, on the prairie north of Winnipeg. They had one child, a seven-year-old boy named Harry. He was a strange child, very small for his age, and shy without being cowardly. He had an odd habit of following dogs, chickens, pigs and birds, imitating their voices and actions with an exactness that onlookers sometimes declared to be uncanny.

One day he had gone quietly after a prairie chicken that kept moving away from him without taking flight, clucking when she clucked, and nodding his head or shaking his 'wings' when she did. So he wandered on and on till the house was hidden from view behind the trees that fringed the river, and the child was completely lost.

There was nothing remarkable in his being away for several hours, but a heavy thunderstorm coming up that afternoon called attention to the fact that the boy was missing, and when the first casual glance did not discover him, it became serious, and a careful search was begun.

Father and mother, with the near neighbours, scoured the prairie till dark, and began the next day at dawn, riding in all directions, calling and looking for signs. After a day or two the neighbours gave it up, believing that the child was drowned and carried away by the river. But the parents continued their search even long after all hope seemed dead. And there was no hour of the day when that stricken mother did not send up a prayer for heavenly help; nor any night when she did not kneel with her husband and implore the one who loved and blessed the babes of Jerusalem to guard her little one and bring him back in safety.

There was one neighbour of the family who joined in the search that had nevertheless incurred the bitter dislike of little Harry Service. The feeling was partly a mere baby instinct, but pointedly because of the man's vicious cruelty to animals, wild or tame, that came within his power. Only a week before he had set steel traps at a den where he chanced to find a pair of badgers in residence. The first night he captured the father badger. The cruel jaws of the jag-toothed trap had seized him by both paws, so he was held helpless. The trap was champed and wet with blood and froth when Grogan came in the morning. Of what use are courage and strength when one cannot reach the foe? The badger craved only a fair fight, but Grogan stood out of reach and used a club till the light was gone from the brave eyes and the fighting snarl was still.

The trap was reset in the sand, and Grogan went. He carried the dead badger to the Service house to show his prize and get help to skin it, after which he set off for the town and bartered the skin for what evil indulgence it might command, and thought no more of the trap for three days. Meanwhile the mother badger, coming home at dawn, was caught by one foot. Strain as she might, that deadly grip still held her; all that night and all the next day she struggled. She had little ones to care for. Their hungry cries from down the burrow were driving her almost mad; but the trap was of strong steel, beyond her strength, and at last the crying of the little ones in the den grew still. On the second day of her torture, the mother in desperation chewed off one of her toes and dragged her bleeding foot from the trap.

Down the burrow she went first, but it was too late: her babies were dead. She buried them where they lay and hastened from that evil spot.

Water was her first need, next food, and then at evening she made for an old den she had used the autumn before.

And little Harry, meanwhile, where was he? That sunny afternoon in June he had wandered away from the house, and losing sight of the familiar building behind the long fringe of trees by the river, he had lost his bearings. Then came the thunder-shower which made him seek for shelter. There was nothing about him but level prairie, and the only shelter he could find was a badger hole, none too wide even for his small form. Into this he had backed and stayed with some comfort during the thunderstorm, which continued till night. Then in the evening the child heard a sniffing sound and a great, grey animal loomed up against the sky, sniffed at the tracks and at the open door of the den. Next it put its head in, and Harry saw by the black marks on its face that it was a badger. He had seen one just three days before. A neighbour had brought it to his father's house to skin it. There it stood sniffing, and Harry, gazing with less fear than most children, noticed that the visitor had five claws on one foot and four on the other, with recent wounds, proof of some sad experience in a trap. Doubtless this was the badger's den, for she – it proved a mother – came in, but Harry had no mind to surrender. The badger snarled and came on, and Harry shrieked, 'Get out!' and struck with his tiny fists, and then, to use his own words, 'I scratched the badger's face and she scratched mine.' Surely this badger was in a generous mood for she did him no serious harm, and though the rightful owner of the den, she went away and doubtless slept elsewhere.

Night came down. Harry was very thirsty. Close by the door was a pool of rainwater. He crawled out, slaked his thirst, and backed into the warm den as far as he could. Then remembering his prayers, he begged God to 'send mamma', and cried himself to sleep. During the night he was awakened by the badger coming again, but it went away when the child scolded it.

Next morning Harry went to the pool again and drank. Now he was so hungry; a few old rose hips hung on the bushes near the den. He gathered and ate these but was even hungrier. Then he saw something moving out on the plain. It might be the badger so he backed into the den, but he watched the moving thing. It was a horseman galloping. As it came nearer Harry saw that it was Grogan, the neighbour for whom he had such a dislike, so he got down out of sight. Twice that morning men came riding by, but having once yielded to his shy impulse, he hid again each time. The badger came back at noon. In her mouth she held the body of a prairie chicken, pretty well plucked and partly devoured. She came into the den sniffing as before. Harry shouted, 'Get out! Go away.' The badger dropped the meat and raised her head. Harry reached and grasped the food and devoured it with the appetite of one starving. There must have been another doorway for later the badger was behind the child in the den, and still later when he had fallen asleep she came and slept beside him. He awoke to find the warm furry body filling the space between him and the wall, and knew now why it was he had slept so comfortably.

That evening the badger brought the egg of a prairie chicken and set it down unbroken before the child. He devoured it eagerly, and again drank from the drying mud puddle to quench his thirst. During the night it rained again, and he would have been cold, but the badger came and cuddled around him. Once or twice it licked his face. The child could not know, but the parents discovered later that this was a mother badger which had lost her brood and her heart was yearning for something to love.

Now there were two habits that grew on the boy. One was to shun the men that daily passed by in their search, the other was to look to the badger for food and protection, and live the badger's life. She brought him food often not at all to his taste—dead mice or ground-squirrels—but several times she brought in the comb of a bee's nest or eggs of game-birds, and once a piece of bread almost certainly dropped on the trail from some traveller's lunch-bag. His chief trouble was water. The prairie pool was down to mere ooze, and with this he moistened his lips and tongue. Possibly the mother badger wondered why he did not accept her motherly offerings. But rain came often enough to keep him from serious suffering.

Their daily life was together now, and with the imitative power strong in all children and dominant in him, he copied the badger's growls, snarls and purrs. Sometimes they played tag on the prairie, but both were ready to rush below at the slightest sign of a stranger.

Two weeks went by. Galloping men no longer passed each day. Harry and the badger had fitted their lives into each other's, and strange as it may seem, the memory of his home was already blurred and weakened in the boy. Once or twice during the second week men had passed nearby, but the habit of eluding them was now in full possession of him.

One morning he wandered a little farther in search of water, and was alarmed by a horseman appearing. He made for home on all fours—he ran much on all fours now—and backed into the den. In the prairie grass he was concealed, but the den was on a bare mound and the horseman caught a glimpse of a whitish thing disappearing down the hole. Badgers were familiar to him, but the peculiar yellow of this and the absence of black marks gave it a strange appearance. He rode up quietly within twenty yards and waited.

After a few minutes the grey-yellow ball slowly reappeared and resolved itself into the head of a tow-topped child. The young man leaped to the ground and rushed forward, but the child retreated far back into the den beyond reach of the man, and refused to come out. Nevertheless there was no doubt that this was the missing Harry Service. 'Harry! Harry! don't you know me? I'm your cousin Jack,' the young man said, in soothing, coaxing tones. 'Harry, won't you come out and let me take you back to mamma? Come, Harry! Look! here are some cookies!' but all in vain. The child hissed and snarled at him like a wild thing, and retreated as far as he could till checked by a turn in the burrow.

Now Jack got out his knife and began to dig until the burrow was large enough for him to crawl in a little way. At once he succeeded in getting hold of the litle one's arm and drew him out struggling and crying. But now there rushed also from the hole a badger, snarling and angry; it charged at the man, uttering its fighting snort. He fought it off with his whip, then swung to the saddle with his precious burden and rode away as for his very life, while the badger pursued for a time. But it was easily left behind, and its snorts were lost and forgotten.

The father was coming in from another direction as he saw this strange sight: a horse galloping madly over the prairie, on its back a young man shouting loudly, and in his arms a small, dirty child, alternately snarling at his captor, trying to scratch his face, or struggling to be free.

The father was used to changing intensity of feeling at these times, but he turned pale and held his breath till the words reached him: 'I have got him, thank God! He's all right,' and he rushed forward shouting, 'My boy! My boy!'

But he got a rude rebuff. The child glared like a hunted cat, hissed at him, and menaced with hands held claw-fashion. Fear and hate were all he seemed to express. The door of the house flung open and the distracted mother, now suddenly overjoyed, rushed to join the group. 'My darling! My darling!' she sobbed, but little Harry was not the same as when he left them. He hung back, he hid his face in the coat of his captor, scratched and snarled like a beast; he displayed his claws and threatened fight, till strong arms gathered him up and placed him on his mother's knees in the old, familiar room with the pictures, and the clock ticking as of old, the smell of frying bacon, and the nearness of his father's form; and above all his mother's arms about him, her magic touch on his brow, and her voice, 'My darling! My darling! Oh, Harry, don't you know your mother? My boy! My boy!' And the struggling little wild thing in her arms grew quiet, his animal anger died away, his raucous hissing gave place to a short panting, and that to a low sobbing that ended in a flood of tears and a passionate 'Mamma, mamma, mamma!' as the veil of a different life was rolled away, and he clung to his mother's bosom.

But even as she cooed to him and stroked his brow and won him back again, there was a strange sound, a snarling hiss at the open door. All turned to see a great badger standing there with its front feet on the threshold. Father and cousin exclaimed, 'Look at that badger!' and reached for the ready gun, but the boy screamed again. He wriggled from his mother's arms and rushing to the door cried, 'My badgie! My badgie!' He flung his arms around the savage thing's neck, and it answered with a low purring sound as it licked its lost companion's face. The men were for killing the badger, but it was the mother's keener insight that saved it, as one might save a noble dog that had rescued a child from the water.

It was some days before the child would let the father come near. 'I hate that man; he passed me every day and would not look at me,' was the only explanation. Doubtless the first part was true, for the badger den was but two miles from the house and the father rode past many times in his radiating search, but the tow-topped head had escaped his eye.

It was long and only by slow degrees that the mother got the story that is written here, and parts of it were far from clear. It might all have been dismissed as a dream or a delirium but for the fact that the boy had been absent two weeks; he was well and strong now except that his lips were blackened and cracked with the muddy water. The badger had followed him home and was now his constant friend.

It was strange to see how the child oscillated between the two lives, sometimes talking to his people exactly as he used to talk, and sometimes running on all fours, growling, hissing and tussling with the badger. Many a game of 'King of the Castle' they had together on the low pile of sand left after the digging of a new well. Each would climb to the top and defy the other to pull him down, till a hold was secured and they rolled together to the level, clutching and tugging, Harry giggling, the badger uttering a peculiar high-pitched sound that might have been called snarling had it not been an expression of good nature. Surely it was a badger laugh. There was little that Harry could ask without receiving it those days, but his mother was shocked when he persisted that the badger must sleep in his bed; yet she so arranged it. The mother would go in the late hours and look at them with a little pang of jealousy as she saw her baby curled up, sleeping soundly with that strange beast.

It was Harry's turn to feed his friend now, and side by side they sat to eat. The badger had become an established member of the family. But after a month had gone by an incident took place that I would gladly leave untold.

Grogan, the unpleasant neighbour, who had first frightened

Harry into the den, came riding up to the Service homestead. Harry was in the house for the moment. The badger was on the sand pile. Instantly on catching sight of it, Grogan unslung his gun and exclaimed, 'A badger!' To him a badger was merely something to be killed. He fired, and the kindly animal rolled over, stung and bleeding, but recovered and dragged herself towards the house. 'Bang!' and the murderer fired again, just as the inmate rushed to the door – too late. Harry ran towards the badger shouting, 'Badgie! My badgie!' He flung his baby arms around the bleeding neck. It fawned on him feebly, purring a low, hissing purr, then mixing the purrs with moans, grew silent, and slowly sank down and died in his arms. 'My badgie! My badgie!' the boy wailed, and all the ferocity of his animal nature was directed against Grogan.

'You'd better get out of here before I kill you!' thundered the father, and the hulking halfbreed sullenly mounted his horse and rode away.

A great part of his life had been cut away, and it seemed as though a deathblow had been dealt the boy. The shock was more than he could stand. He moaned and wept all day, he screamed into convulsions, he was worn out at sundown and slept little that night. Next morning he was in a raging fever and ever he called for 'My badgie!' He seemed at death's door the next day, but a week later he began to mend and in three weeks was as strong as ever and childishly gay, with occasional spells of sad remembering that gradually ceased.

He grew up to early manhood in a land of hunters, but he took no pleasure in the killing that was such sport to his neighbours' sons, and to his dying day he could not look on the skin of a badger without feelings of love, tenderness, and regret.

Grumphie *by F G Turnbull*

Since the appearance of Grumphie at the last cattle show at Kirkbracken, pigs have acquired a new significance in that locality. No longer are they regarded merely as potential rashers, but also as creatures of unusual character and temperament. This state of affairs, however, is due less to the illustrious pig itself than to the tremendous efforts of Tam and Wullie Donaldson, the boys who reared it. Tam and Wullie are the twin sons of the postman, who since the great event has viewed his progeny with mixed feelings of pride and uncertainty. The lads are twelve years old, red-polled, and magnificently freckled.

The affair began when the flooded Ericht river brought Grumphie, then about the size of a rabbit, and sent him whirling half-drowned into a creek where the boys were paddling. Of course they salvaged the pig, and, when its owner could not be traced, claimed the booty.

Sandy Petrie, the farmer of Bannockbrae, offered to provide accommodation for the foundling—an offer which was gladly accepted. And the farmer gave things a send-off when he suggested facetiously that Tam and Wullie should send their pig to the cattle show, due to take place some months later.

Naturally enough, the boys decided that this was a whale of a notion, and they had their own ideas of how a pig should be reared and prepared for prize-winning. As Tam expressed it: 'It has tae be terrible clean an' awfu' fat.' And the fact that Sandy Petrie was to show a pig of his own introduced the competitive touch that inspired the pair to mighty, if unusual, effort.

Operations commenced when the twins arrived at Bannockbrae one Saturday morning bearing a pail, scrubbing brush, and a piece of perfumed soap wherewith to wash their pig.

Little Grumphie squealed his protest at the first touch of the water; he squirmed and fought, but the twins persisted, although when smothered in suds the pig was as slippery as an eel. However, the victim quietened down quickly and inexplicably, submitting without further struggle to the novel treatment.

After the first application of the brush, Wullie turned to the pail for more water, then he searched about his feet for something.

'Where's the soap?' he asked.

His brother looked around, but the soap had vanished. Presently Tam's inquiring eye lit on Grumphie's face. The little creature was munching busily with a look of supreme bliss on his funny features. White froth dripped from his jaws. Tam crouched to sniff it.

'Great Pete!' he said. 'Lily o' the Valley! The wee beggar's eaten the soap!'

'Hevvins!' gasped Wullie, utterly appalled.

For several moments the twins stared in open-mouthed astonishment, marvelling at the appetite of their pet. Only a few minutes earlier he had had a meal of jawsticker toffee, carrots, potatoes and turnip. But their thoughts were rudely interrupted when Grumphie suddenly uttered a hoarse squeak of dismay and became violently sick.

Somewhat chastened by this experience, Grumphie had not the heart or energy to struggle as his toilet was completed. Then Tam began to collect the washing material. Once more he searched about his feet, then he asked abruptly: 'Where's the brush!'

Instantly Wullie's eyes turned in consternation on Grumphie.

'Hevvins!' he again exclaimed. 'Dinna tell me he's eaten it! That's apple, spuds, carrots, turnip, jawsticker, soap, an' now a scrubbin' brush. Gosh! What a stummick!'

But to their intense relief the boys found the brush jammed in the underside of the pail.

As the weeks went by heaven on earth was Grumphie's lot.

He was stuffed with foods of every description, and attention such as no pig had ever known before was lavished on him. Wullie attended to his feeding and the sty, while Tam attended to his toilet.

Tam's especial pride was Grumphie's peerless tail. It was an absolute gem, he thought—the curliest a pig ever wore. The tuft of pale yellow hair on the end of it was washed, brushed and combed regularly, and encouraged by such solicitude it lengthened considerably. But the soap had to be chosen with discretion. The perfumed variety was hopeless, it possessed such a fascination for the pig. So eager was he to eat it, the twins dared not put it down within his reach. As a susbstitute they tried carbolic, and Grumphie's interest in the soap immediately waned.

Later, as his weight and strength increased, the pig began to assert his independence. He accepted his mighty meals as his birthright, but he began to take exception to the washing. Whereupon he developed a fraction of his lazy brain to deal with the situation, and kicked the water pail over whenever he saw it. When the lads countered this move by placing the pail on the low sty roof, Grumphie refused to stand still; he raced screeching round the sty with the twins and the brush in pursuit.

'Och, this'll no' dae!' panted Wullie one morning after a strenuous and vain pursuit. 'We'll have to tie him up.'

Tam agreed. 'I'll tell ye,' he said. 'Let's shove his tail through yon wee hole in that board an' tie a knot on the other side.'

After a herculean struggle the twins managed to poke Grumphie's tail through the hole, but found that the thing would not tie in a knot. So a piece of thin rope was attached to it by a cunning hitch, and a stone on the other end of the rope anchored the rebellious porker securely to the sty wall. He uttered blood-curdling shrieks and pulled with all his might, but the rope would not break, nor would his tail tear out at the roots.

The washing proceeded, and when the pig received his final

wipe down the rope was removed. With a surly grunt of relief Grumphie waddled towards his food trough, and as he did so a look of horror overspread the faces of the twins. They stared as though hypnotized at the stern of their pig.

In his struggle to escape he had straightened his tail. Gone was the curl that had delighted the hearts of his owners. The appendage stuck out and upwards, stiff as a poker, whilst the drooping pennant of hair at the end accentuated its oddity. Tam was on the verge of tears.

'Look,' he said. 'After a' my brushin' an' combin', we've gone an' took the spring oot o' it.'

'Ay,' added Wullie, gloomily, 'an' a pig withoot a curly tail is as much use at a show as a hedgehog is in your bed. That's done it noo.'

But having gone so far with the preparation of their pet, the lads could not let a straightened tail baulk them of a possible prize. Presuming that the sinews were strained, they borrowed some embrocation from Sandy Petrie and proceeded to anoint Grumphie's rudder. They rubbed and rubbed, letting the tail go now and then to see whether it would assume its earlier curl. But no. It remained as stiff as ever, without the least suspicion of a twist.

The treatment was repeated at intervals for a week, without success. In desperation Tam suggested that they thread the tail through a coiled length of lead gas pipe. The pipe was obtained and the stubborn tail pulled through it with a string, then the whole spectacular arrangement was firmly fastened to Grumphie's rear.

Three days later, with bated breath, the boys removed the pipe, screwing it off carefully so that a possible new curl might not be disturbed. But the confounded thing seemed straighter than ever. It was then coiled round and round a thin stick and tightly bound with string. This device also failed in its object, and the heartbroken twins concluded that the glory had departed for ever from the plumpest end of Grumphie.

While they sat and stared despondently at the pig a large blue fly whizzed round and round, then lit on Grumphie's back. Wullie flicked it away and scratched the spot where it had landed. And to the unbounded delight and astonishment of the boys, the obstinate tail slowly but surely assumed its normal curl.

For a long, breathless moment Tam and Wullie gazed pop-eyed at the miracle, then, throwing himself on his knees beside the pig, Tam looked with moist affection into Grumphie's bleary eyes and said:

'Weel, noo; there's a real, clever auld beast. Ye deserve a—' His voice trailed away in dismay. That brute of a tail had gone and straightened out again.

Wullie wondered if the scratching, which Grumphie had always enjoyed, had anything to do with it. Again he rubbed his fingers along the rough hide, and in immediate response the tail curled up once more. He ceased rubbing, and the tail poked out again. This was terrific. The next five minutes were spent in intermittent scratchings and hilarious laughter as the remarkable tail popped out and in.

'By gosh, this is something like a pig!' said Tam with enthusiasm. 'All we have tae do tae mak' him curl his tail at the show is just tae scratch his back. Hooray, we'll get a prize wi' him yet!'

The evening before the show was an awful experience for Grumphie. He was scrubbed and scoured until he was almost skinned. Then to ease his hurt feelings he was given the mightiest meal of all. Here was consolation. Life, he felt, still had its points.

While he devoured his food, Tam seated himself in the rear to devote his attention to the hair on the porker's tail. He teased it out, brushed it tenderly, then applied brilliantine and screwed it up in a curling-pin. The captivating odour of the dressing wafted to Grumphie's nose. He sniffed, and traced it to its source, but was much too fat to bend far in the middle, and so was denied the privilege of a chew at his own tail. Life lost a point.

While the pig cleaned the corners of his trough, his proud owners wondered if there was anything further they could do to enhance his appearance. Tam studied the toe of his boot while considering, and there he found inspiration.

'Wullie!' he exclaimed. 'What about blackenin' his trotters wi' boot polish. They'd show up a lot better than they dae noo.'

'Great idea,' agreed Wullie. 'We'll dae just that. An' Mr. Petrie says we can get a cart specially for him in the mornin', so we'll tie him up in paper tae keep him clean on the road.'

The twins arrived at the show next day in a downpour of rain. The judges had decided that in view of the weather all those animals that could walk should be brought into the ring under cover for judging. So the twins left Grumphie in the cart with a cover to keep him dry until it was his turn to appear, and they went inside to witness the parade of animals.

The ring where the judging took place was surrounded by tiers of seats where farmers and their friends sat discussing and criticizing the entries. With them sat Tam and Wullie, until it was announced that the pigs would now come in. They waited near the door to hear their number called. It was 23 — the last on the list. In the interval Sandy Petrie had spoken to the judges, warning them that the final exhibit was something of a novelty, and he related its history.

When the second last number was reached the twins dashed out and unwrapped their pet. Wullie brushed his bristles until they shone, and Tam removed the curling-pin from his tail. They were polishing his blackened feet with their handkerchiefs when a raucous voice bawled: 'Number Twenty-three.'

'Come on; oot wi' ye!' urged the lads excitedly. With a grunt of relief the pig leapt heavily from the cart, and guiding him carefully, the twins drove him towards the ring. At ever other step they glanced at his tail. It was tightly curled. There was a toffee apple in his mouth. Then into the ring marched the postman's sons and their pig.

A murmur of surprise and amusement arose from the assembled farmers as the trio came in. This was followed by a ripple of laughter when the black trotters were noticed, and the beautifully waved tail. The boys blushed furiously.

'Umph!'

Grumphie uttered a grunt of disapproval. Apparently he disliked noisy crowds, and to express his feelings he unwound his tail and stuck it straight out. A gale of laughter greeted this feat, but it was nothing to the roar of approval that arose when Tam, with a look of desperation, seized the offending object and tried to curl it up again.

With the pig in his present humour it was like trying to put a curl in rubber. The thing sprang out straight immediately the boy released it. At this the audience was convulsed with mirth.

Seeing the state of affairs, Wullie began to scratch the pig's thick neck energetically with one hand and to stroke the underside of his fat tummy with the other. Rummaging frantically in his pocket, Tam produced another toffee apple and rammed it into the sulky porker's mouth.

By a storm of hand-clapping the farmers showed their appreciation of this cunning move. But Grumphie refused to respond. He wanted to get out of here, and no amount of scratching or toffee would make him curl his rudder if he didn't want to.

Meanwhile Tam wrought manfully. Now and again when he had pushed it in, the tail would remain coiled for an instant. And, watching it like a hawk, he knelt with upheld hands ready to push it in again should the infernal thing shoot out.

The judges leaned against the railings and howled. Never in all their lives had they seen anything like this. The pig was almost hidden from sight by the boys who tried so desperately to make it happy. The farmers roared with delight; tears of joy streamed down their weather-beaten faces. They hadn't enjoyed anything so much since the day when a stallion bit the judge's ear off.

The officials held a quick consultation, then the leading judge stifled his laughter and addressed the boys.

'If only your pig had a permanent curl in his tail,' he said, 'he would have got a prize. He's a magnificent specimen except for that one flaw.'

The twins looked at each other in despair. Then suddenly Tam bawled:

'Wullie; bolt oot an' get a cake o' scented soap.'

A tremendous yell from the audience followed this extraordinary command, and a loud cheer accompanied Wullie's exit.

'If yer honours'll wait just one wee minnit,' said Tam pleadingly to the judges, 'we'll put a better curl in Grumphie's tail than ye ever saw before.'

Hearing Tam's plea, the judges looked inquiringly at one another and nodded.

Three minutes later Wullie dashed into the ring, tearing the wrapping from a tablet of highly perfumed soap. He flopped down on his knees in front of the disgruntled animal and held out the offering.

'Here: eat it, ye stubborn brute,' he growled savagely.

'Now then, Grumphie,' wheedled Tam, 'ye're a fine pig. Will ye no' curl your bonny tail up? I'll feed ye on jawsticker and scented soap as lang as ye live if ye dae.'

Grumphie sniffed the Lily of the Valley, then with a grunt of pleasure he opened his mouth and engulfed the titbit. And now the show, prizes, competition and everything else were forgotten as every eye focused on Grumphie's tail. Slowly it began to bend, then with a gay whirl it assumed the tightest curl that ever adorned the blunt end of a pig.

The result was pandemonium. Cheer upon cheer rang out, and wild, insistent cries of 'Special! Special! Special!' And in response to the general demand the judges decided to award the twins a special prize for their remarkable pig. A fresh burst of cheering greeted the announcement, and with freckled, beaming faces the boys looked up to the audience.

The leading judge called to his clerk for a 'special' ticket, and the gaily coloured card was handed to him. In honour of the occasion the official determined to add a longer length of string and hang the card round Grumphie's neck himself. Down he crouched before the pig and reached out his hands to fasten the string round the fat neck.

Suddenly Grumphie emitted a queer, gurgling sound:

'Uuuumph, grumph, aaaouwp!' Tam and Wullie danced on their toes, yelling frantically.

'Look oot, yer honour: *he's goin' tae be sick!*'

The next instant Grumphie proved it, and in a mighty bound the judge hurled himself to the railings out of the way. Twenty seconds later, helpless with mirth, the audience saw Grumphie pick up his prize card and devour it with every sign of satisfaction. And in a resounding thunder of applause, Tam and Wullie drove Grumphie out of the ring.

Rats *by J B S Haldane*

Once upon a time there was a man called Smith. He was a greengrocer and lived in Clapham. He had four sons. The eldest was called George, after the king, and it was arranged that he was to inherit his father's shop. So at school he went to special botany classes, and learned about the hundred and fifty-seven different kinds of cabbage, and the forty-four sorts of lettuce. And he went to zoology classes and learned about the seventy-seven kinds of caterpillar that live in cabbages, and how the green kind come out if you sprinkle the cabbages with soapy water, and the striped ones with tobacco juice, and the big fat brown ones with salt water. So when he grew up he was the best greengrocer in London, and no one ever found caterpillars in his cabbages.

But Mr Smith only had one shop, so his other three sons had to seek their own fortunes. The second son was called Jim, but his real name was James, of course. He went to school and he won all the prizes for English essays. He was captain of the school soccer team, and played half-back. And he was very clever at all sorts of tricks, and used to play them on the masters. One day he stuck a match-head into the chalk. It wasn't a safety-match head either, but one of those blue and white ones that strike on anything. So when the master started writing on the board he struck the match, and nobody did much work for the next five minutes. Another day he put methylated spirits in the ink-pots, and the ink wouldn't stick to the pens. It took the master half-an-hour to change all the ink, so they didn't get much French done that hour, and he hated French, anyway. But he never did ordinary tricks like putting putty in the keyholes or dead rats on the master's desk.

The third son was called Charles, and he was fairly good at mathematics and history, and got into the cricket eleven as a slow left-handed bowler; but the only thing he was really good at was chemistry. He was the only boy in his school (or in any other, for all I know) who had ever made paradimethylaminobenzaldehyde or even arabitol (which is really quite hard to make, and has nothing to do with rabbits). He could have made the most awful smells if he had wanted to, because he knew how. But he was a good boy and didn't. Besides, if he had they might have stopped him doing chemistry, and he wanted to go on doing chemistry all his life.

The fourth son was called Jack. He wasn't much good at any of his lessons, nor at games either. He never managed to kick a ball straight, and he went to sleep when fielding at cricket. The only thing he was any good at was wireless. He made pretty well everything in the set at home, except the valves, and he was learning to make them when the story begins. He had a great-aunt called Matilda who was so old that she said she could remember the railway from London to Dover being built. She couldn't walk, and had to stay in bed all the time. He made her earphones to listen with, and she said she hadn't been so happy since Queen Victoria's time. Jack was very clever with other electrical things too. He made a special dodge to get electric light for his father's house without paying for it, and the meter didn't register anything for a week. Then his father found out what was happening and said, 'We mustn't do that, it's stealing from the electric light company.' 'I don't think it's stealing,' said Jack. 'A company isn't a person, and besides the electricity goes through our lamps and back again to the main. So we don't keep it, we only borrow it.' But his father made him take his gadget down, and even paid the company for the current, for he was an honest man.

Mr Smith had a daughter named Lucille, but everyone called her Pudgy. She doesn't really come into the story, so I shan't say anything more about her till the end, except that when she was little her front teeth stuck out; but in the end they managed to push them in.

Now at this time there was a great plague of rats in the

London Docks. They were specially fierce rats, whose ancestors had come on steamers from Hong Kong along with tea and ginger and silk and rice. These rats ate all sorts of food which are brought to London in ships because we cannot grow enough food in England to feed all the people there. They ate wheat from Canada and cheese from Holland and mutton from New Zealand and beef from Argentina. They bit out pieces from the middle of Persian carpets to line their nests, and wiped their feet on silk coats from China.

Now the man who is at the head of all the docks in London is called the Chairman of the Port of London Authority, and he is a very big bug indeed. He has an office near Tower Hill that is almost as big as Buckingham Palace. He was awfully angry about the rats, because he has to look after the cargoes that are brought in ships from the time they are unloaded till they are taken away in trains and lorries and carts. So he had to pay for the things the rats ate. He sent for the best rat-catchers in London. But they only caught a few hundred rats, because they were a very cunning kind of rat. They had a king who lived in a very deep hole, and the othe rats brought him specially good food. They brought him chocolate that had come from Switzerland, bits of turkey from France, dates from Algiers, and so on. And he told the other rats what to do. If any rat got caught in a trap, he sent out special messengers to give warning of the danger. He had an army of ten thousand of the bravest young rats, and they used to fight any other animals that were sent against them. A terrier can easily kill one or two rats; but if a hundred rush at him all at once, he may kill three or four of them, but the others will kill him in the end. The rats with the toughest teeth were trained to be engineers, and used to bite through the wire of rat-traps to let prisoners out.

So in one month these rats killed a hundred and eighty-one cats, forty-nine dogs and ninety-five ferrets. And they wounded a lot of others so badly that they ran away if they even smelt a rat, let alone saw one. And they let out seven hundred and forty-two prisoners from six hundred and eighteen traps. So the rat-catchers lost their best dogs and ferrets and traps, and gave up the job in despair. The people in the docks sent round to the chemists' shops for all sorts of rat poison, and sprinkled it about mixed with different sorts of bait. But the king rat gave orders that none of his subjects were to eat food unless it came straight out of a box or a barrel or a bag. So only a few disobedient rats got poisoned, and the others said it served them right. And the poison was no more use than the dogs and ferrets and traps.

So the Chairman of the Port of London Authority called a meeting of the Authority in the great Board Room of his office, and said, 'Can you suggest what is to be done about the rats?' So the Vice-Chairman suggested putting an advertisement in the papers. The next week advertisements came out in all the papers. It was on the front page of the ones that have the news inside, like *The Times* and the *Daily Mail,* and in the middle of the ones that have the news outside, like the *Daily Herald* and the *Evening Standard.* It took up a whole page and was printed in huge letters, so that almost everyone in England read it. All the Smith family read it except great-aunt Matilda, who never read the papers because she listened in to all the broadcast news.

Now this advertisement made all the competitions in the papers look pretty silly. For the Chairman of the Port of London Authority offered a hundred thousand pounds and his only daughter in marriage to the man who would rid the docks of rats. (If the winner was married already, of course he wouldn't be allowed to marry the daughter, but he got a diamond bracelet for his wife as a consolation prize.) There was a photograph of the hundred thousand pounds; and they were real golden sovereigns, not paper notes. And there was a photograph of the daughter, who was very pretty, with short curly golden hair and blue eyes. Besides this, she could play the violin, and had won prizes for cookery, swimming and figure skating. The only snag was that the competitors had to bring their own things for killing the rats so really it cost a lot of money to go in for the competition.

Still thousands and thousands of people went in for it. They had to get three extra postmen to take the letters to the Chairman the next morning. And so many people rang him up on the telephone that the wires melted. For months and months all sorts of people tried their luck. There were chemists and magicians, and bacteriologists and sorcerers, and zoologists and spiritualists and lion hunters, but none of them was able to kill more than a few rats. What was worse, they interfered with the unloading of the ships, and quite a lot of corn had to be sent round by Liverpool and Cardiff and Hull and Southampton instead of London.

Among the people who tried their luck were Jim, Charles and Jack Smith. Jim thought that if only he could make a trap that looked quite ordinary, he would be able to fool the rats, just as he used to fool the masters at school. Now he knew that there were all sorts of old tins lying about the docks, so he designed a special sort of trap made from an old tin. The rats smelt the bait inside and jumped onto the top. But the top was a trap-door, and so the rat fell through and couldn't get out again. He spent all his spare time making these traps and he got his friend to help. He borrowed ten pounds from his father, and got Bill Johnson, who was an out-of-work tinsmith, to make more for him. In the end he had one thousand three hundred and ninety-four of these traps; but seventeen of them were pretty bad, so he didn't bring them.

He went along to Tower Hill with his traps on one of his father's carts, and saw the vice-chairman, who was a duke, and was looking after all the rat-catching. The vice-chairman said, 'Of course these traps aren't enough to go all around all the docks, but we will try them on one.' So they tried them on the West India Dock, where the ships come from Jamaica and the other islands round it with sugar and rum and treacle and bananas. I don't think that was a very good place to choose, because the rats there are specially quick and nimble. This is because they are constantly tumbling into barrels and vats and hogsheads and demijohns of treacle. The slow ones get stuck in it and that is the end of them. Only the quick ones escape. So all the rats round there are very quick, and good climbers.

Half Jim's traps were baited with cheese and half with bacon. The first night they caught nine hundred and eighteen rats. Jim was terribly pleased, and thought he was going to win the prize. But the next night they only caught three rats, and the third only two. The king rat had warned all his subjects to avoid tins, and only stupid or disobedient ones got caught. On the fourth night they moved the traps to the Victoria Docks, but they only caught four rats. The warning had been spread. So Jim went home very sad. He had wasted a lot of time and ten pounds, and the other boys at school called him Tinned Rats.

Charles Smith had quite a different scheme. He invented a special kind of poison with no taste or smell. I am not going to tell you what it was, or how to make it, because some murderer might read this story, and use it to kill all sorts of people. He made a lot of this poison, and he also made a lot of stuff that gives the smell to Roquefort cheese, which is a very cheesy kind of cheese made in France. This is called methyl-hepta-decyl ketone, and I think it has a lovely smell. Some other people don't like it, but rats do. He borrowed twenty pounds from his father, and got a hundred cheap and nasty cheeses. Then he cut each into a hundred bits. He soaked them first in the poison, and then in the stuff with the Roquefort smell, and put them into ten thousand cardboard boxes. He thought that if he did that the rats would not think that they were ordinary poisoned bait, which is just scattered about, and not in boxes at all. But the boxes were cardboard, so that the rats could get in quite easily.

All through one day two men with wheelbarrows went round the docks, leaving the ten thousand cheese boxes in different places. And Charles went behind them with a squirt, and squirted the cheesy stuff over them. The whole of East London smelt of cheese that afternoon. When the sun set, the rats came out, and they said to one another, 'This must be a marvellous cheese, quite a little box of it smells as much as a whole case of ordinary cheeses.' So a great many of them ate it. They even brought some back to the king rat. But luckily for him he had just had a huge meal of walnuts and smoked salmon and wasn't hungry. The poison took some time to work, and it wasn't until three o'clock in the morning that the rats began to die of it. The king at once suspected the cheese, and sent out messengers to warn his subjects against it.

Also there was a wicked rat which had been sentenced to death for eating its own children, and the king made it eat the bit of cheese that had been brought him. When it died he knew the cheese was poisoned, and sent out another lot of messengers. The next morning they picked up four thousand five hundred and fourteen dead rats, and ever so many more were dead in their holes, besides others that were ill. The Chairman was so pleased that he gave Charles the money to buy another lot of cheeses. But when, two days later, they left them about, only two out of eight thousand boxes had been opened. So they knew the rats had been too clever for them again. Charles was very sad indeed. He had been so sure of success that he had ordered a wedding ring for his marriage with the Chairman's daughter, and written to the Archbishop of Canterbury to marry them. Now he had to write to the jeweller and the Archbishop to say he wasn't going to marry after all. And worst of all, the cheesy smell stuck to him for a month. They wouldn't have him back at school, and he had to sleep in the coal shed at home.

Last of all Jack tried his plan. It needed a lot of money, and though he borrowed thirty pounds from his father, it was not enough. But he borrowed some more from me, and sold some wireless sets that he had made, until he gradually got all he needed. He bought some very fine iron filings, much finer than the ordinary kind, and had them baked into biscuits. The biscuits were left about the docks. At first the rats would not touch them, but later they found they did them no harm, and began to eat them. Meanwhile Jack got seven perfectly enormous electro-magnets, which were put in different docks. Each was in the middle of a deep pit with smooth sides. And cables were laid so that current from the District Railway and the East London Railway could be put through the magnets. Luckily Jack knew the head electrical engineer on the underground railways, because they were both keen on wireless, so he was able to arrange to borrow their current. When he thought that the rats had eaten enough iron filings he made arrangements to turn the current through the magnets. All loose iron, steel, or nickel things had to be tied up. And the ships, because they are made of steel and iron, had to be tied up very tight indeed with extra cables. And all the people in the docks that night had to wear special boots or shoes with no nails in them; except the vice-chairman who was a duke, so of course he had gold nails in his boots.

At half-past one in the morning the last underground railway train had stopped, and they turned all the current that had been working the trains into the first magnet. A few rusty nails and tin cans came rushing towards it, and so did the rats, but more slowly. They were full of iron filings, and the magnet just pulled them. Soon the hole round that magnet was full of rats, and they switched the current on to the next magnet. Then they turned on the third magnet, and so on. Of course only the rats that were above ground were pulled into the holes by the magnets. But they turned them on again and again, and as more and more came out of their holes they were caught too.

The king rat knew something was going wrong, and felt himself pulled to one side of his hole. He sent out messengers but they never came back. At last he went out himself, and a magnet pulled him into one of the pits. When morning came they turned on water taps and drowned all the rats that had been caught by the magnets. These rats weighed a hundred and fifty tons. No-one ever counted them, but they reckoned to have caught three-quarters of a million.

There were some awkward accidents. A night-watchman called Alf Timmins had forgotten to wear boots without nails. So the magnet pulled him along feet first. He managed to get his boots off just as he was on the edge of the rat pit, but a rat hung on to each of his toes, and the magnet pulled these rats so hard that all his toes came off. So now he has no toes, like the Pobble, and takes a smaller size in boots than he used to. But another watchman called Bert Higgs had better luck. Before the war he had been a great billiard-player, but he got a bit of a shell into his brain, and couldn't play billiards any more. And none of the doctors could get the bit out. So when Jack turned the magnet on, the bit of shell came popping out of his head, and the part of his brain that made him so good at billiards started working again. So now he is billiard-champion of Poplar.

The next night they turned on the magnets again, and caught a lot more rats, about a hundred tons. Their king was dead, so they didn't know what to do. The third night they caught a lot more again. After that the few rats that were left were so frightened that they all ran away. Some got onto ships and went abroad. Some went into London, and were a great nuisance to the people there, but none stayed in the docks. They caught none the fourth night, and though they hunted with dogs and ferrets the next day, there wasn't a rat in the place.

So Jack Smith got the hundred thousand pounds and married the Chairman's daughter on a ship at sea. He didn't want to be married in church, and he thought registrars' offices were ugly, so he hired a ship, and when they were three miles from shore the captain married them, which he couldn't have done if they had been only two-and-a-half miles away, because that is the law. They had two boys and two girls, and Jack got a very good job with the BBC as an engineer. With all that money he might have lived all his life without doing any work, but he was so fond of wireless that he wanted to go on working at it.

His sister married the duke, so she is a duchess; but of course duchesses aren't so important now as they used to be. She has diamond heels to her shoes to match her husband's gold nails. He gave his brothers Jim and Charles money to start in their professions. So Jim spent it on magic wands and trick hats and tables, and became a conjurer, and a very good one too. And Charles went to the university and became a professor of chemistry. I am a professor too, and I know him quite well. So they all lived happily ever after.

Lost and Found *by Stuart Cloete*

Groot Hendrik Marais of Sterkfontein in the Waterberg—one of the finest farms in South Africa—was depressed. He was convinced that his youngest son Japie, the apple of his eye, was mad. Not seriously mad, but just mad enough to make him completely inexplicable. A boy like no other boy that he or anyone else had ever seen in these parts. He filled his pipe slowly, stuffing down the Boer tobacco—home-grown naturally—with an enormous thumb, lit it and put on the metal cap that prevented its popping out when it took. He stared at his feet. They were very big, too.

He himself had made the *veldschoens* he wore out of the skins of his own beasts. Shoemaking was one of his hobbies. He had five children, so with himself and his wife there were fourteen shoes to make and keep in repair. That was another thing. Japie would not wear shoes. Not ever. Not even on Sunday. Of course most children ran about on the farm barefooted, but he felt that they should wear shoes on Sundays and when they went into the dorp—the little township of Boomspruit. It was respectable. After all, they were not poor whites, and besides he liked people to see how well he made shoes. It gave him great pleasure to brey the skins, to cut them and fit them. *Ja*, he made the children's shoes, and his wife cut their nails—finger and toenails.

One day she had said, 'Hendrik, do you know how many nails I cut today?'

He had said, 'No. How should I know? That is for women.'

And she had said, 'One hundred.'

It had surprised him to find out how many fingers and toes his children had. But he worked it out. Ten toes and ten fingers each—that was twenty. Five times twenty was a hundred. *Ja*, she was right, as usual. Of course the bigger ones could cut their own, but they didn't, or if they did they did not do so to his wife's satisfaction. She liked things well done and so for that matter did he.

He brought his mind to Japie. He must talk to Jacoba about him. He screwed up his courage at last and said:

'I believe that our Japie is mad. I can find no other explanation for his behaviour. *Ja*,' he said, 'it's a fine thing, my heart, that we should have four fine children and that the fifth, at the age of six, goes mad.'

'*Nee*, Hendrik,' his wife said, 'our Japie is not mad.'

'Not mad? Just look at the cats we have. Ten cats and every one brought home by Japie. *Magtig*,' he said, 'in a place where there are no cats he finds one and comes back with it in his arms.'

'There are no mice,' his wife said.

'No mice! Does it take ten cats to have no mice? And the oxen? Why did he let the oxen out of the kraal and into the mealies?'

'I asked him,' his wife said.

'*Ja*, you asked him, and what did he say?'

'He said, "Ma, the oxen looked so sad and they said, 'please Japie, let us out and into the lovely green mealies'." '

'That proves what I said. He is mad. A son who talks to the oxen and does what they say. And he used to be such a good boy.'

'He's still a good boy,' Mevrou Marais said. 'It's just that he loves too much. He wants everyone to be happy.'

'What about me? When the oxen eat my mealies does that make me happy? A son who prefers the oxen to his pa?'

'It's his character, Hendrik. He is a character that boy. He takes after you. You are a character. All the world says "that Groot Hendrik Marais—what a character he is".'

Hendrik banged his cup on the table. '*Magtig*, I am fifty years old. I can be a character. But what will become of the world if children of six are characters? And what about the time he came home naked carrying his clothes after a big rain, with us worrying about him, thinking he might be drowned in the spruit or struck by lightning?'

'He looked so sweet,' Jacoba said. '*Ja*, he looked like a little angel—except for the wings—standing there in the doorway.'

'Give me more coffee,' Hendrik said, 'before I go mad too.' He gulped the coffee and said, 'I suppose he told you about that, too?'

'*Ja*, he told me.'

'What did he say?'

'He said he knew I got worried about him getting wet and he thought it was because of his clothes being spoiled, so he took them off and hid them in an old ant heap. Then he sat down and waited for the rain to stop. He knew it would not last. Then he got them out and decided that it felt nice to be naked on the veld and that the sun was nice and warm on his body, and by that time he was so nearly home that it did not seem worth putting them on, since it was nearly dark and almost time for bed. He is a very intelligent child, Hendrik.'

'*Ja*, so intelligent he will send me mad too. Send us all mad. And now I am going out to the lands to grow more mealies and sweet potatoes and kaffir-corn so that Japie can let the oxen out to eat them as soon as they are ready to reap.'

'He says that the oxen ploughed the land and harrowed it, and planted the mealies and cultivated them, and therefore should have some of the produce of the land, Hendrik.'

But when she looked up Jacoba found she was talking to herself. Her husband had disappeared. This did not stop her and she continued, 'It is his sense of justice. *Magtig*, that child should be a lawyer. *Ja*, a lawyer of six years old, that's our Japie.'

Japie, hidden under the long folds of the green tablecloth where he was playing at being in a tent, agreed with his mother. He knew he was intelligent and just. That he would have a great future. That he was special, a law unto himself, and in no way resembled his brothers and sisters who, though so much older than he, the eldest being twelve, were without any real intelligence or sense of adventure. In fact they bored him. He loved his mother who was the source of all food and comfort and stood between him and the world—a soft cushion between him and reality. His father, Groot Hendrik, he loved also, but in the way one loved God with whom he was somewhat confused owing to his size, his great voice, and his big grey and yellow beard. His father was authority, and when each morning he read aloud the word of God it seemed to Japie that it was He who was speaking. God in his father's form or his father in God's.

What astonished him about all grown-up people was their skill and strength, the things they knew and could do. It was, for instance, wonderful to be able to make shoes. But with this wonder went a surprise at their lack of wisdom and understanding. Even his mother could not understand his relationship with the animals with whom he had long and involved conversations. The oxen, the horses, the dogs, the cats, chickens, ducks, geese, turkeys, guinea fowl, even the bees all had things to tell him. The wild birds, too, and the beetles and things that crawled over the veld. Even the lizards and the snakes all had their own ways of expressing themselves and none were to be feared provided they understood that you loved them as brothers. The great charm of their conversation was that it was silent or almost silent. They did not chatter like other children. You knew from listening to a dog that he was hunting, that he had treed something and needed help, that he was lonely, that he was angry at a stranger coming near the house. And the cats. How many things they could say, talking not only with their voices, but with their eyes, their ears and the way they moved their tails. He loved cats because they were, like himself, so filled with love. So filled that sometimes it seemed to him they would burst with their purring affection.

But now the big thing on his mind was this trip that was under discussion. The whole family were going to a big political meeting in the truck. They were taking a tent, food and cooking pots, and were going to camp there for a week. This was the biggest thing that had happened in his life and he tried to visualize it. There would be a great many people, uncountable numbers, all strangers except those who had come like his own family from Boomspruit and the Waterberg, many of whom he would know. There would be bands and merry-go-rounds—a funfair with sideshows of bearded women, two-headed calves, mermaids and other wonders of which he had heard. There would be many small children with whom he would play instead of being by himself all the time, or tagging along behind his brothers and sisters.

He thought about all this until the coast was clear and his mother went out to look for an egg a cackling hen had just laid. She liked to collect eggs. It took her out of the kitchen into the yard and a few hens stole back to their nests when she went out and watched them coming into the open from some bush or secret place where they had planned to raise a family.

It did not matter how often he told the hens to stay quiet. 'Why must you make all that noise,' he said, 'when you have laid an egg? Is it so wonderful? Every hen lays eggs, so why are you so vain that you must tell the world?' But they never listened to him and so his mother found their nests and took their eggs, substituting a china one for the one she had taken. He had told them this too, but they loved their china eggs and brooded them as stupidly as girls nursing their dolls as if they were real children. Of all the animals and birds he knew there was the least to be gained from discussing anything with chickens. Ducks were much more intelligent. It was really a waste of time to talk to a hen.

At last the great day came. The truck was loaded. The children, all dressed in their best clothes, sat on the big rolled tent. There were hampers of food, baskets of eggs, bottles of home-brewed peach brandy, jars of *konfyt*, Pa's rifle—for there would be shooting competitions—some of Ma's embroidery, for the ladies would compete too in such feminine arts, carefully wrapped in crinkly tissue.

All this Japie had watched big-eyed, enthralled. Somehow in his mind it was confused with the flight of the Jews from Egypt, the great Exodus, the years in the wilderness also, but more vaguely, with Gabriel blowing his trumpet and driving Adam and Eve forth from the garden. This was when Pa blew the horn for them all to mount the truck. Suddenly the future seemed less bright, more dangerous, and home and the cats and dogs, even the chickens—stupid as they were—more than ever beautiful.

Now they were off, and in the excitement of travel, of the dust that rose in clouds, the new country, the other cars and wagons they passed, all fear was lost. This was adventure.

They stopped once to eat by the roadside, then they went on and Japie slept with his head in his mother's lap. Then they were there. The tent was raised by a big blue-gum. His pa made a fire. Ma and Susanna and Fredrika cooked the dinner. He hurried himself to sleep to make tomorrow come quicker.

With the first dawn Japie was up, crying out for breakfast so that he could be off, so that day could really begin. At last it was over. His mother had changed his shirt and trousers, washed his face once more, combed his yellow hair into a crest like a cockscomb, and told him to be a good boy and not get lost. Then she had forgotten him in the press of events—there were the other children to see to, there were people coming and going.

Get lost, indeed! Were they mad, all these people? Even his pa and ma, to think he could get lost when they were camped by a big blue-gum—far the biggest for miles around.

Japie was enjoying himself. He had had no idea that there were so many people in the world. In his life he had seen about three hundred people—the whole population of Boomspruit when they came to church on Sunday or to the fair or the circus. They had, till now, represented the total population of the world, which ended as far as he was concerned with the Waterberg in the south and the Zoutpansberg in the north. But this was wonderful, this new world of strange legs and skirts. He moved among them as if they were a forest of moving trees. He stared with large blue eyes at everything. He stared at a young woman who was eating pink sweets till she gave him one and stroked his head. He did not care for being stroked but he liked sweets. Then a man gave him a balloon—a red balloon. He had never seen a balloon before. He held it on its string for a while. It tugged at his fingers as if it wanted to be free, so he let it go. He wanted the balloon to be happy too. It went up and up into the blue sky, floating beautifully till it got quite small and disappeared.

He thought, 'Now it is happy.' Nothing should be tied, restrained, all things should be free—even children. That was why he was so happy himself. Here he was in this moving leg forest, as free as a bird on the veld.

He stood at the entrance of the sideshow tent. People were going in and coming out. He went in with some others but he was stopped by a man who wanted money.

'I have no money, *meneer*,' he said. 'I do not wish to buy anything, only to see.'

A big man said, 'You want to see the bearded lady?'

'Ja, *meneer*,' he said, 'but I have no money.'

The man took his hand and led him in, paying a shilling for him. The man explained that bearded ladies were very rare which was why it cost a shilling to see one.

Japie said, 'My pa has a beard, a long yellow beard. My pa is Groot Hendrik. You have heard of him, I expect?'

The man laughed and said, '*Ja*, naturally I have heard of him. All the world knows of Groot Hendrik.'

Japie said, '*Ja, meneer*,' because all the world had heard of his pa.

The bearded lady looked just like a lady with a beard.

Then a great voice which was like the voice of God roared over the air. 'Attention!' it said. 'Attention, please! A little boy is lost. If he is found please take him to the Red Cross tent. His name is Japie Marais. He is six years old and is wearing a white shirt, khaki shorts and no shoes. He has blond hair and blue eyes.'

This made Japie laugh. How odd that a boy of his own name should be lost. But of course, Japie was a common name and there were many Marais. His walk now had an object. It would be nice to find his little cousin, a boy of his own age and name, and play with him. I will seek him, he thought, and to every small boy he saw he said, 'Are you by any chance my cousin Japie Marais who is lost?'

He found several small boys called Japie and several called Marais but no Japie Marais. He found a black and white collie pup that was half-grown, which followed him after they had had some conversation together.

He said, 'Dog, you look sad and bedraggled. Perhaps you are lost like the small boy I am seeking.'

The dog said, 'No. I am not lost. I am abandoned. I need a home and a master.'

'You have found both,' Japie said. 'Come, let us go on together.'

He found a lady's handbag which someone had dropped which he would give to his pa who would find its rightful owner, and all the time he wondered about this lost child, this other Japie, thinking how awful it must be to be lost. He must come from the dorp, he thought, for no country boy could be lost here.

Then the radio blared out again. 'Will anyone who knows the whereabouts of Japie Marais, six years old, wearing a white shirt, khaki shorts and no shoes, report to the Red Cross tent? . . . Lost—a boy six years old answering to the name of Japie Marais . . . Report to the Red Cross tent . . . Repeat—the Red Cross tent . . . Japie Marais . . . six years old . . . no shoes . . . white shirt, khaki shorts . . .'

How odd that this cousin should be his own age and dressed exactly as he was. This struck Japie as a very satisfactory coincidence. We shall have a lot in common, he thought.

A big man who smelled of horses and tobacco put his hand on Japie's shoulder. 'And what are you doing, *jong*, all by yourself?'

'Me?' Japie said. 'Why, I'm looking for my cousin, Japie Marais, who has got himself lost.'

'Small boys do get lost, you know,' the man said.

'Only if they are from the dorp, *meneer*. Us country boys can find our way around. My pa is camped by the big blue-gum that is standing by itself. My pa is Groot Hendrik of the

Waterberg. Everyone knows him. He can do everything better than any other man.'

'I'm sure he can,' the man said, taking his hand.

'Now shall we see if your cousin is on the merry-go-round?'

'You think he might be?' Japie said hopefully. 'Man, I should like to find him so that we could play together. You see, my brothers are too big for me. At least they say I am too small.'

'That is something quite different, *jong*.'

'*Ja, meneer*,' Japie said. 'It is not my fault I am small. It is just that I am young. *Ja*,' he said, 'I am six. But I shall grow.' He stood with his legs apart, his bare dirty brown toes planted in the dust of the fairground. 'I am the son of Groot Hendrik and I shall be big too one day.'

The man led him on towards the loud music that came from the merry-go-round. The animals—horses, giraffes, ostriches and zebras—went round and round and up and down.

'Can I ride a zebra?' Japie said.

'*Ja*, you can ride anything you want.' The man bought a ticket and gave it to an attendant who lifted Japie up on the back of the zebra as soon as it came to a stop.

'I can see far from here,' Japie said, as he stared about him, 'but I do not see any other little boy dressed like me, *meneer*.' Then he said, 'Will you hold my dog? He will try to follow me.'

'*Ja*, I will hold him.' The man bent down and picked up the collie pup.

This was a fine sensation, going round and round past all the staring people and up and down like a horse jumping, only of course, there were no jumps. Each time he went round Japie waved to the big man and the dog in his arms. When he came to a stop at last the man put the pup down. It ran to Japie and stood with its paws on his shoulders and licking his face.

'He loves you,' the man said.

'*Ja*,' Japie said. 'He is a very loving dog and thank you very much, sir. *Baie dankie*, very thank you, *meneer*. We must now continue our search for Japie, because his parents will be very anxious if I do not find him soon.'

Then he saw a small girl in a blue dress crying. She had long black hair and sobbed bitterly. She had no handkerchief so Japie went up to her and lent her his after he had removed his treasures from it. They consisted of a broken padlock, a bit of string, the *voorslag* of a whip, a mouse skull, two marbles and the remains of a sweet he had been sucking when the lady in pink had given him a fresh one.

He wiped the little girl's face and asked her name.

'I am Maria,' she said, 'and I am four years old, and I am lost.'

'Never mind, Maria,' he said. 'I will take care of you. You just come with me. We will see everything and then I will take you to my pa. He will find your pa. *Ja*,' he said, 'there is nothing my pa cannot do. He is Groot Hendrik Marais, a man well known all over the world.' He pushed the half-sucked sweet into her mouth, gave her the lady's handbag to carry like a grown-up and followed by the collie pup they wandered through the crowd.

Maria said, 'Where are we going, Japie?'

'We are going to see the world, its wonders, and at the same time to find my cousin Japie who is lost.'

'What does he look like?' the little girl asked.

Japie said, 'He is six years old with blue eyes, fair hair, no shoes, and is dressed in a white shirt and khaki shorts.'

Maria looked at him. 'Why,' she said, 'he must be very like you.'

'*Ja*, Maria, that's it. That's why I want to find him. He has my name too. He is my cousin and we could play together.'

'We can all play together,' Maria said. 'Of course I am only a girl and smaller than you, but I play well and will do just what you say.'

Japie stopped and kissed her. 'You are a nice girl,' he said. 'We will play together till we find my cousin. Then we will all play.'

'I can run fast,' Maria said.

'We will run races,' Japie said, 'and because you are smaller and a girl we will give you a big start. That will make it fair. There must be justice. That is what my pa, Groot Hendrik, always says.'

Maria began to cry again. 'I want my pa and ma. I am hungry.'

'That's nothing,' Japie said. 'Come.' He led her to a group of people sitting on the veld eating sandwiches. He went up to a big fat woman and said, '*Tante* auntie, this little girl is hungry. Will you give us some food?'

The woman laughed and then everyone laughed, and she said, 'Sit.'

They sat with the others and were given cups of coffee and sandwiches and sausages. When he had eaten as much as he could, Japie said, 'Are there any scraps over for my dog?'

'What is his name?' the woman asked.

'His name?' Japie said. He thought for a moment and then said, 'His name is Job, for he has had many troubles.'

'And yours?' the woman said.

Japie said, 'I am Japie and I am seeking my cousin Japie Marais who is lost in this great crowd. Is that not a terrible thing for a child?'

A man with his mouth full of sausage said, 'We heard that over the radio. Perhaps he is found by now.'

'I do not know,' Japie said, 'but we will continue to seek him. And now, *baie dankie*,' he said. 'We must go now and find this lost boy.'

He took Maria's hand, and followed by the collie pup was soon lost in the crowd.

They walked on hand in hand till Maria said she was tired.

'*Ja*,' Japie said, 'I am tired too. Not very tired but a little tired, so we shall find a place to rest.'

Before long he saw some forage piled up near two wagons, and leading Maria to it made a nest in the hay for them both. They lay down together and the collie curled up beside them. It was very peaceful and pleasant in the hay. For a little while Japie worried about the lost boy but then decided that he must be safe by now. He closed his eyes and slept. When they awoke it was late afternoon, and Japie said, 'Now we will go and find my pa. You will see then that with him there is nothing to fear. He will find your pa and the owner of the bag.'

'And Job?' Maria said. 'Did you not find him too?'

'Job is different,' Japie said. 'I did not find Job. He found me.'

'Tell me about Job,' Maria said.

'Job is in the Bible,' Japie said. 'Only yesterday my pa read about him to us. He had many troubles that the Lord sent upon him to try him.'

'What is try, Japie?'

'I do not know,' Japie said. 'I think it is what happens when things go wrong.'

'Like me being lost?' Maria said. 'The Lord is trying me?'

'*Ja*, Maria, that's what it is, I think, but when we find my pa he will tell us.'

He pulled her to her feet and brushed the hay out of her hair and off her blue dress with his hand. 'Now we will go,' he said.

And they set off for the big blue-gum where his father's car was parked.

When they got near the tent Japie saw his sister Susanna. He waved to her. She rushed into the tent and shouted, 'Ma! Pa! There he is. There's Japie coming. He has a dog and a little girl with him.' Then she ran towards him, her hair flying out behind her.

'Where have you been, Japie? The whole world has been looking for you. How did you get lost?'

'*Ja*, how did you get lost?' his father said, swinging him up on his shoulder. 'I have been looking everywhere and just came back to tell your ma that I was going to the police again to see if they had found you.'

'Lost?' Japie said. He had his hand fast in his father's beard. 'Lost? Me lost? No,' he said. 'I was not lost. I was looking for that poor little boy, our cousin Japie Marais, who is lost. I thought how worried his pa and ma would be with a small boy like that lost among so many people. I could not find him, Pa.

But I found Maria. She is lost and I said you would find her pa and ma. I also found Job. At least he found me, and I love him. And I love Maria too and I found a handbag.'

'Japie,' his mother said, taking him from his father, 'Japie, did you not hear on the radio about Japie Marais being lost?'

'*Ja*,' he said. 'That's why I took so long. I was seeking him. Then I found Maria. She was hungry so we got some food. Then she was sleepy so we slept. Then we looked some more but failed to find Japie, so we came back.'

'Japie,' she said, 'you were looking for Japie?'

'*Ja*,' he said, 'for Japie Marais, my cousin.'

'*Magtig*,' his father said. 'Japie looking for Japie. *Ons* Japie looking for himself.'

'For me?' Japie said. 'How could it have been me? I was never lost.' He put his arm around Maria and kissed her. The pup stood up on his hind legs and licked the faces of the children.

Japie said, 'Pa, if Maria is really lost, can we keep her? I love her.'

'And Job?' Hendrik asked.

'*Ja*, Job too. I love him.'

'Come,' Hendrik said, 'we will eat. Then I will find the parents of Maria and take the handbag to the police.'

He turned to Jacoba and said, 'Jacoba, you are right again. Our Japie is not mad. It is just that he loves too much.'

The Parsley Garden *by William Saroyan*

One day in August Al Condraj was wandering through Woolworth's without a penny to spend when he saw a small hammer that was not a toy but a real hammer and he was possessed with a longing to have it. He believed it was just what he needed by which to break the monotony and with which to make something. He had gathered some first-class nails from Foley's Packing-House where the boxmakers worked and where they had carelessly dropped at least fifteen cents' worth. He had gladly gone to the trouble of gathering them together because it had seemed to him that a nail, as such, was not something to be wasted. He had the nails, perhaps a half-pound of them, at least two hundred of them, in a paper bag in the apple box in which he kept his junk at home.

Now, with the ten-cent hammer he believed he could make something out of box-wood and the nails, although he had no idea what. Some sort of a table perhaps, or a small bench.

At any rate he took the hammer and slipped it into the pocket of his overalls, but just as he did so a man took him firmly by the arm without a word and pushed him to the back of the store into a small office. Another man, an older one, was seated behind a desk in the office, working with papers. The younger man, the one who had captured him, was excited and his forehead was covered with sweat.

'Well,' he said, 'here's one more of them.'

The man behind the desk got to his feet and looked Al Condraj up and down.

'What's *he* swiped?'

'A hammer.' The young man looked at Al with hatred. 'Hand it over,' he said.

The boy brought the hammer out of his pocket and handed it to the young man, who said, 'I ought to hit you over the head with it, that's what I ought to do.'

He turned to the older man, the boss, the manager of the store, and said, 'What do you want me to do with him?'

'Leave him with me,' the older man said.

The younger man stepped out of the office, and the older man sat down and went back to work. Al Condraj stood in the office fifteen minutes before the older man looked at him again.

'Well,' he said.

Al didn't know what to say. The man wasn't looking at him, he was looking at the door.

Finally Al said, 'I didn't mean to steal it. I just need it and I haven't got any money.'

'Just because you haven't got any money doesn't mean you've got a right to steal things,' the man said. 'Now, does it?'

'No, sir.'

'Well, what am I going to do with you? Turn you over to the police?'

Al didn't say anything, but he certainly didn't want to be turned over to the police. He hated the man, but at the same time he realized somebody else could be a lot tougher than he was being.

'If I let you go, will you promise never to steal from this store again?'

'Yes, sir.'

'All right,' the man said. 'Go out this way and don't come back to this store until you've got some money to spend.'

He opened a door to the hall that led to the alley, and Al Condraj hurried down the hall and out into the alley.

The first thing he did when he was free was laugh, but he knew he had been humiliated, and he was deeply ashamed. It was not in his nature to take things that did not belong to him. He hated the young man who had caught him and he hated the manager of the store who had made him stand in silence in the office so long. He hadn't liked it at all when the young man had said he ought to hit him over the head with the hammer.

He should have had the courage to look him straight in the eye and say, 'You and who else?'

Of course he *had* stolen the hammer and he had been caught, but it seemed to him he oughtn't to have been so humiliated.

After he had walked three blocks he decided he didn't want to go home just yet, so he turned around and started walking back to town. He almost believed he meant to go back and say something to the young man who had caught him. And then he wasn't sure he didn't mean to go back and steal the hammer again, and this time *not* get caught. As long as he had been made to feel like a thief anyway, the least he ought to get out of it was the hammer.

Outside the store he lost his nerve, though. He stood in the street looking in for at least ten minutes.

Then, crushed and confused and now bitterly ashamed of himself, first for having stolen something, then for having been caught, then for having been humiliated, then for not having guts enough to go back and do the job right, he began walking home again, his mind so troubled that he didn't greet his pal Pete Wawchek when they came face to face outside Graf's Hardware.

When he got home he was too ashamed to go inside and examine his junk, so he had a long drink of water from the faucet in the back yard. The faucet was used by his mother to water the stuff she planted every year: okra, bell-peppers, tomatoes, cucumbers, onions, garlic, mint, eggplants and parsley.

His mother called the whole business the parsley garden, and every night in the summer she would bring chairs out of the house and put them around the table she had had Ondro, the neighbourhood handyman, make for her for fifteen cents; and she would sit at the table and enjoy the cool of the garden and the smell of the things she had planted and tended.

Sometimes she would even make a salad and moisten the flat old-country bread and slice some white cheese, and she and he would have supper in the parsley garden. After supper she would attach the water hose to the faucet and water her plants and the place would be cooler than ever and it would smell real good, real fresh and cool and green, all the different growing things making a green-garden smell out of themselves and the air and the water.

William Saroyan

After the long drink of water he sat down where the parsley itself was growing and he pulled a handful of it out and slowly ate it. Then he went inside and told his mother what had happened. He even told her what he had *thought* of doing after he had been turned loose: to go back and steal the hammer again.

'I don't want you to steal,' his mother said in broken English. 'Here is ten cents. You go back to that man and you give him this money and you bring it home, that hammer.'

'No,' Al Condraj said. 'I won't take your money for something I don't really need. I just thought I ought to have a hammer, so I could make something if I felt like it. I've got a lot of nails and some box-wood, but I haven't got a hammer.'

'Go buy it, that hammer,' his mother said.

'No,' Al said.

'All right,' his mother said. 'Shut up.'

That's what she always said when she didn't know what else to say.

Al went out and sat on the steps. His humiliation was really beginning to hurt now. He decided to wander off along the railroad tracks to Foley's because he needed to think about it some more. At Foley's he watched Johnny Gale nailing boxes for ten minutes, but Johnny was too busy to notice him or talk to him, although one day at Sunday School two or three years ago Johnny had greeted him and said, 'How's the boy?' Johnny worked with a box-maker's hatchet and everbody in Fresno said he was the fastest boxmaker in town. He was the closest thing to a machine any packing-house ever saw. Foley himself was proud of Johnny Gale.

Al Condraj finally set out for home because he didn't want to get in the way. He didn't want somebody working hard to notice that he was being watched and maybe say to him, 'Go on, beat it.' He didn't want Johnny Gale to do something like that. He didn't want to invite another humiliation.

On the way home he looked for money but all he found was the usual pieces of broken glass and rusty nails, the things that were always cutting his bare feet every summer.

When he got home his mother had made a salad and set the

table, so he sat down to eat, but when he put the food in his mouth he just didn't care for it. He got up and went into the three-roomed house and got his apple box out of the corner of his room and went through his junk. It was all there, the same as yesterday.

He wandered off back to town and stood in front of the closed store, hating the young man who had caught him, and then he went along to the Hippodrome and looked at the display photographs from the two movies that were being shown that day.

Then he went along to the public library to have a look at all the books again, but he didn't like any of them, so he wandered around town some more, and then around half-past eight he went home and went to bed.

His mother had already gone to bed because she had to be up at five to go to work at Inderrieden's, packing figs. Some days there would be work all day, some days there would be only half a day of it, but whatever his mother earned during the summer had to keep them the whole year.

He didn't sleep much that night because he couldn't get over what had happened, and he went over six or seven ways by which to adjust the matter. He went so far as to believe it would be necessary to kill the young man who had caught him. He also believed it would be necessary for him to steal systematically and successfully the rest of his life. It was a hot night and he couldn't sleep.

Finally, his mother got up and walked barefooted to the kitchen for a drink of water and on the way back she said to him softly, 'Shut up.'

When she got up at five in the morning he was out of the house, but that had happened many times before. He was a restless boy, and he kept moving all the time every summer. He was making mistakes and paying for them, and he had just tried stealing and had been caught at it and he was troubled. She fixed her breakfast, packed her lunch and hurried off to work, hoping it would be a full day.

It was a full day, and then there was overtime, and although she had no more lunch she decided to work on for the extra money, anyway. Almost all the other packers were staying on, too, and her neighbour across the alley, Leeza Ahboot, who worked beside her, said, 'Let's work until the work stops, then we'll go home and fix a supper between us and eat it in your parsley garden where it's so cool. It's a hot day and there's no sense not making an extra fifty or sixty cents.'

When the two women reached the garden it was almost nine o'clock, but still daylight, and she saw her son nailing pieces of box-wood together, making something with a hammer. It looked like a bench. He had already watered the garden and tidied up the rest of the yard, and the place seemed very nice, and her son seemed very serious and busy. She and Leeza went straight to work for their supper, picking bell-peppers and tomatoes and cucumbers and a great deal of parsley for the salad.

Then Leeza went to her house for some bread which she had baked the night before, and some white cheese, and in a few minutes they were having supper together and talking pleasantly about the successful day they had had. After supper they made Turkish coffee over an open fire in the yard. They drank the coffee and smoked a cigarette apiece, and told one another stories about their experiences in the old country and here in Fresno, and then they looked into their cups at the grounds to see if any good fortune was indicated, and there was: health and work and supper out of doors in the summer and enough money for the rest of the year.

Al Condraj worked and overheard some of the things they said, and then Leeza went home to bed, and his mother said, 'Where you get it, that hammer, Al?'

'I got it at the store.'

'How you get it? You steal it?'

Al Condraj finished the bench and sat on it. 'No,' he said, 'I didn't steal it.'

'How you get it?'

'I worked at the store for it,' Al said.

'The store where you steal it yesterday?'

'Yes.'

'Who give you job?'

'The boss.'

'What you do?'

'I carried different stuff to the different counters.'

'Well, that's good,' the woman said. 'How long you work for that little hammer?'

'I worked all day,' Al said. 'Mr Clemmer gave me the hammer after I'd worked one hour, but I went right on working. The fellow who caught me yesterday showed me what to do, and we worked together. We didn't talk, but at the end of the day he took me to Mr Clemmer's office and he told Mr Clemmer that I'd worked hard all day and ought to be paid at least a dollar.'

'That's good,' the woman said.

'So Mr Clemmer put a silver dollar on his desk for me, and then the fellow who caught me yesterday told him the store needed a boy like me every day, for a dollar a day, and Mr Clemmer said I could have the job.'

'That's good,' the woman said. 'You can make a little money for yourself.'

'I left the dollar on Mr Clemmer's desk,' Al Condraj said, 'and I told them both I didn't want the job.'

'Why you say that?' the woman said. 'Dollar a day for eleven-year-old boy good money. Why you not take job?'

'Because I hate the both of them,' the boy said. 'I would never work for people like that. I just looked at them and picked up my hammer and walked out. I came home and I made this bench.'

'All right,' his mother said. 'Shut up.'

His mother went inside and went to bed, but Al Condraj sat on the bench he had made and smelled the parsley garden and didn't feel humiliated any more.

But nothing could stop him from hating the two men, even though he knew they hadn't done anything they shouldn't have done.

Luke Baldwin's Vow
by Morley Callaghan

That summer when twelve-year-old Luke Baldwin came to live with his Uncle Henry in the house on the stream by the sawmill, he did not forget that he had promised his dying father he would try to learn things from his uncle; so he used to watch him very carefully.

Uncle Henry, who was the owner of the sawmill, was a big, burly man weighing more than sixteen stone, and he had a rough-skinned, brick-coloured face. He looked like a powerful man, but his health was not good. He had aches and pains in his back and shoulders which puzzled the doctor.

The first thing Luke learned about Uncle Henry was that everybody had great respect for him. The four men he employed in the sawmill were always polite and attentive when he spoke to them. His wife, Luke's Aunt Helen, a kindly, plump, straightforward woman, never argued with him. 'You should try and be like your Uncle Henry,' she would say to Luke. 'He's so wonderfully practical. He takes care of everything in a sensible, easy way.'

Luke used to trail round the sawmill after Uncle Henry not only because he liked the fresh clean smell of the newly-cut wood and the big piles of sawdust, but because he was impressed by his uncle's precise, firm tone when he spoke to the men.

Sometimes Uncle Henry would stop and explain to Luke something about a piece of timber. 'Always try to learn the essential facts, son,' he would say. 'If you've got the facts, you know what's useful and what isn't useful, and no-one can fool you.'

He showed Luke that nothing of value was ever wasted around the mill. Luke used to listen, and wonder if there were another man in the world who knew so well what was needed and what ought to be thrown away.

Uncle Henry had known at once that Luke needed a bicycle to ride to his school, which was two miles away in town, and he bought him a good one. He knew that Luke needed good, serviceable clothes. He also knew exactly how much Aunt Helen needed to run the house, the price of everything, and how much a woman should be paid for doing the rough housework. In the evenings Luke used to sit in the sitting-room watching his uncle making notations in a black notebook which he always carried in his vest pocket, and he knew that he was assessing all the transactions of the day.

Luke promised himself that when he grew up he too would be admired for his good, sound judgment. But, of course, he couldn't always be watching and learning from Uncle Henry, for too often when he watched him he thought of his own father: then he was lonely. So he began to build up another secret life for himself at the sawmill, and his companion was the eleven-year-old collie, Dan, a dog blind in one eye and with a slight limp in his left hind leg.

Dan was a fat, slow-moving old dog. He was very affectionate and his eye was the colour of amber. His fur was amber too. When Luke left for school in the morning, the old dog followed him for half a mile down the road, and when he returned in the afternoon there was Dan waiting at the gate.

Sometimes they would play round the millpond or by the dam, or go down the stream to the lake. Luke was never lonely when the dog was with him. There was an old rowing boat they used as a pirate ship in the stream, and they would be pirates together, with Luke shouting instructions to Captain Dan and with the dog seeming to understand and wagging his tail enthusiastically. Its amber eye was alert, intelligent and approving. Then they would plunge into the copse on the other side of the stream, pretending they were hunting tigers. Of course, the old dog was no longer much good for hunting: he was too slow and too lazy. Uncle Henry no longer used him for hunting rabbits or anything else.

When they came out of the copse, they would lie together on the cool, grassy bank being affectionate with each other, with

Luke talking earnestly, while the collie, as Luke believed, smiled with the good eye. Lying in the grass, Luke would say things to Dan he could not say to his uncle or aunt. Not that what he said was important; it was just stuff about himself that he might have told to his own father or mother if they had been alive. Then they would go back to the house for lunch, and after lunch Dan would follow him down the road to Mr Kemp's house, where they would ask old Mr Kemp if they could go with him to round up his four cows. The old man was always glad to see them. He seemed to like watching Luke and the collie pretending they were cowboys.

Uncle Henry no longer paid much attention to the collie, though once when he tripped over him on the verandah, he shook his head and said thoughtfully, 'Poor old fellow, he's through. Can't use him for anything. He just eats and sleeps and gets in the way.'

One Sunday during Luke's summer holidays when they had returned from church and had had their lunch, they all moved out to the verandah where the collie was sleeping. Luke sat down on the step, his back against the verandah post. Uncle Henry took the rocking chair, and Aunt Helen stretched herself out in a deck-chair, sighing contentedly. Then Luke, eyeing the collie, tapped the step with the palm of his hand, giving three little taps like a signal and the old collie, lifting his head, got up stiffly with a slow wagging of the tail as an acknowledgment that the signal had been heard, and began to cross the verandah to Luke.

But the dog was sleepy; his bad eye was turned to the rocking chair; in passing, his left front paw went under the rocker. With a frantic yelp, the dog went bounding down the steps and hobbled round the corner of the house, where he stopped, hearing Luke coming after him. All he needed was the touch of Luke's hand. Then he began to lick the hand methodically, as if apologizing.

'Luke,' Uncle Henry called sharply, 'bring that dog here.'

When Luke led the collie back to the verandah, Uncle Henry nodded and said, 'Thanks, Luke.' Then he took out a cigarette, lit it, put his big hands on his knees and began to rock in the chair while he frowned and eyed the dog steadily. Obviously he was making some kind of important decision about the collie.

'What's the matter, Uncle Henry?' Luke asked nervously.

'That dog can't see any more,' Uncle Henry said.

'Oh yes, he can,' Luke said quickly. 'His bad eye got turned to the chair, that's all, Uncle Henry.'

'And his teeth are gone, too,' Uncle Henry went on, paying no attention to what Luke had said. Turning to the deck-chair he called, 'Helen, sit up a minute, will you?'

When she got up and stood beside him, he went on, 'I was thinking about this old dog the other day, Helen. It's not only that he's just about blind, but did you notice that when we drove up after church he didn't even bark?'

'It's a fact he didn't, Henry.'

'No, not much good even as a watchdog now.'

'Poor old fellow. It's a pity, isn't it?'

'And no good for hunting. He eats a lot, I suppose.'

'About as much as he ever did, Henry.'

'The plain fact is the old dog isn't worth his keep any more. It's time we got rid of him.'

'It's always so hard to know how to get rid of a dog, Henry.'

'I was thinking about it the other day. Some people think it's best to shoot a dog. I haven't had any cartridges for that shotgun for over a year. Poisoning is a hard death for a dog. Perhaps drowning is the easiest and quickest way. Well, I'll speak to one of the mill hands and get him to look after it.'

Crouching on the ground, his arms round the old collie's neck, Luke cried out, 'Uncle Henry, Dan's a wonderful dog! You don't know how wonderful he is!'

'He's just a very old dog, son,' Uncle Henry said calmly. 'The time comes when you have to get rid of any old dog. We've got to be practical about it. I'll get you a pup, son. A smart little dog that'll be worth its keep. A pup that will grow up with you.'

'I don't want a pup!' Luke cried, turning his face away.

57

Circling round him, the dog began to bark, then flick his long pink tongue at the back of Luke's neck.

Aunt Helen, catching her husband's eye, put her finger on her lips, warning him not to go on talking in front of the boy.

But Luke was frightened, for he knew what his uncle was like. He knew that if his uncle had decided that the dog was useless and that it was sane and sensible to get rid of it, he would be ashamed of himself if he were diverted by any sentimental considerations. Luke knew in his heart that he couldn't move his uncle. All he could do, he thought, was to keep the dog away from his uncle, keep him out of the house, feed him when Uncle Henry wasn't about.

Next day at noon Luke saw his uncle walking from the mill towards the house with old Sam Carter, a mill hand. Sam Carter was a dull, stooped, slow-witted man of sixty with an iron-grey beard. He hardly ever spoke to anybody.

Watching from the verandah, Luke noticed that his uncle suddenly gave Sam Carter a cigarette, which Sam put in his pocket. Luke had never seen his uncle give Sam a cigarette or pay much attention to him.

Then, after lunch, Uncle Henry said lazily that he would like Luke to take his bicycle and go into town and get him some tobacco.

'I'll take Dan,' Luke said.

'Better not, son,' Uncle Henry said. 'It'll take you all afternoon. I want that tobacco. Go along, Luke.'

His uncle's tone was so casual that Luke tried to believe they were not merely getting rid of him. Of course he had to do what he was told. He had never dared to refuse to obey an order from his uncle. But when he had taken his bicycle and had ridden down the lane that followed the stream to the main road and had got about a quarter of a mile along the road, he found that all he could think of was his uncle handing old Sam Carter the cigarette.

Slowing down, sick with worry now, he got off the bike and stood uncertainly on the sunlit road. Sam Carter was a gruff, aloof old man who would have no feeling for a dog. Then suddenly Luke could go no farther without getting some assurance that the collie would not be harmed while he was away. Across the fields he could see the house.

Leaving the bike in the ditch, he started to cross the fields, intending to get close enough to the house so Dan could hear him if he whistled softly. He got about fifty yards away from the house and whistled and waited, but there was no sign of the dog.

For a few minutes Luke couldn't make up his mind what to do, then he decided to go back to the road, get on his bike and go back the way he had come until he got to the place where the lane joined the road. There he could leave his bike, go up the lane, then into the tall grass and get close to the front of the house and the sawmill without being seen.

He had followed the drive for about a hundred yards, and when he came to the place where the river began to bend sharply towards the house his heart fluttered and his legs felt paralysed, for he saw the old boat in the one place where the river was deep, and in the boat was Sam Carter with the collie.

The bearded man in the blue overalls was smoking the cigarette; the dog, with a rope round its neck, sat contentedly beside him, its tongue going out in a friendly lick at the hand holding the rope. It was all like a crazy dream picture to Luke: all wrong because it looked so lazy and friendly, even the curling smoke from Sam Carter's cigarette.

But as Luke cried out, 'Dan, Dan! Come on, boy!' and the dog jumped at the water, he saw that Sam Carter's left hand was hanging deep in the water, holding a foot of rope with a heavy stone at the end. As Luke cried out wildly, 'Don't! Please don't!' Carter dropped the stone, for the cry came too late: it was blurred by the screech of the big saws at the mill. But Carter was startled, and he stared stupidly at the riverbank, then he ducked his head and began to row quickly to the bank.

But Luke was watching the collie take what looked like a long, shallow dive, except that the hind legs suddenly kicked up above the surface, then shot down, and while he watched,

Luke sobbed and trembled, for it was as if the happy secret part of his life round the sawmill was being torn away from him. But even while he watched, he seemed to be following a plan without knowing it, for he was already fumbling in his pocket for his jack-knife, jerking the blade open, kicking his shoes off while he muttered fiercely and prayed that Sam Carter would get out of sight.

It hardly took the mill hand a minute to reach the bank and go slinking furtively round the bend as if he felt the boy was following him. But Luke hadn't taken his eyes off the exact spot in the water where Dan had disappeared. As soon as the mill hand was out of sight, Luke slid down the bank and took a leap at the water, the sun glistening on his slender body, his eyes wild with eagerness as he ran out to the deep place, then arched his back and dived, swimming under water, his open eyes getting used to the greenish-grey haze of the water, the sandy bottom and the imbedded rocks.

His lungs began to ache, then he saw the shadow of the collie floating at the end of the taut rope, rock-held in the sand. He slashed at the rope with his knife. He couldn't get much strength in his arm because of the resistance of the water. He grabbed the rope with his left hand, hacking with his knife. The collie began to drift up slowly, like a water-soaked log. Then his own head shot above the surface, and while he was sucking in the air he was drawing the rope, pulling the collie towards him and treading water. In a few strokes he was away from the deep place and his feet touched the bottom.

Hoisting the collie out of the water, he scrambled towards the bank, lurching and stumbling in front because the collie felt like a dead weight.

He went on up the bank and across the path to the tall grass, where he fell flat, hugging the dog and trying to warm him with his own body. But the collie didn't stir, the good amber eye remained closed. Then suddenly Luke wanted to act like a resourceful, competent man.

Getting up on his knees, he stretched the dog out on its

belly, drew him between his knees, felt with trembling hands
for the soft places on the flanks just above the hipbones, and
rocked back and forth, pressing with all his weight, then
relaxing the pressure as he straightened up. He hoped that he
was working the dog's lungs like a bellows. He had read that
men who had been thought drowned had been saved in this
way.

'Come on, Dan. Come on, old boy,' he pleaded softly. As a
little water came from the collie's mouth, Luke's heart jumped,
and he muttered over and over, 'You can't be dead, Dan! You
can't, you can't! I won't let you die, Dan!' He rocked back and
forth tirelessly, applying the pressure to the flanks. More water
dribbled from the mouth. In the collie's body he felt a faint
tremor. 'Oh gosh, Dan, you're alive,' he whispered. 'Come on,
boy. Keep it up.'

With a cough the collie suddenly jerked his head back, the
amber eye opened, and there they were looking at each other.
Then the collie, thrusting his legs out stiffly, tried to hoist
himself up, staggered, tried again, then stood there in a stupor.
He shook himself like any other wet dog, turned his head, eyed
Luke, and the red tongue came out in a weak flick at Luke's
cheek.

'Lie down, Dan,' Luke said. As the dog lay down beside
him, Luke closed his eyes, buried his head in the wet fur and
wondered why all the muscles of his arms and legs began to
jerk in a nervous reaction now that it was all over.

'Stay there, Dan,' he said softly, and went back to the path,
got his shoes and came back beside Dan and put them on. 'I
think we'd better get away from this spot, Dan,' he said. 'Keep
down, boy. Come on.' And he crawled on through the tall
grass till they were about seventy-five yards from the house.
There they lay down together.

In a little while he heard his aunt's voice calling, 'Luke. Oh,
Luke! Come here, Luke!'

'Quiet, Dan,' Luke whispered. A few minutes passed, and
then Uncle Henry called, 'Luke, Luke!' and he began to come
down the path. They could see him standing there, massive

and imposing, his hands on his hips as he looked down the path, then he turned and went back to the house.

As he watched the sunlight shine on the back of his uncle's neck, the exultation Luke had felt at knowing the collie was safe beside him turned to bewildered despair, for he knew that even if he should be forgiven for saving the dog when he saw it drowning, the fact was that his uncle had been thwarted. His mind was made up to get rid of Dan, and in a few days' time, in another way, he would get rid of him, as he got rid of anything at the mill that he believed to be useless or a waste of money.

As he lay back and looked up at the hardly-moving clouds, he began to grow frightened. He couldn't go back to the house, nor could he take the collie into the woods and hide him and feed him there unless he tied him up. If he didn't tie him up, Dan would wander back to the house.

'I suppose there's just nowhere we can go, Dan,' he whispered sadly. 'Even if we start off along the road, somebody will see us.'

But Dan was watching a butterfly that was circling crazily above them. Raising himself a little, Luke looked through the grass at the corner of the house, then he turned and looked the other way to the wide blue lake. With a sigh he lay down again, and for hours they lay there together, until there was no sound from the saws in the mill and the sun moved low in the western sky.

'Well, we can't stay here any longer, Dan,' he said at last. 'We'll just have to get as far away as we can. Keep down, old boy,' and he began to crawl through the grass, going farther away from the house. When he could no longer be seen, he got up and began to run across the field towards the road leading to town.

On the road the collie would turn from time to time as if wondering why Luke shuffled along, dragging his feet wearily, his head down. 'I'm stumped, that's all, Dan,' Luke explained. 'I can't seem to think of a place to take you.'

When they were passing the Kemps' house they saw the old

man sitting in the garden, and Luke stopped. All he could think of was that Mr Kemp had liked them both and it had been a pleasure to help him fetch the cows in the evening. Dan had always been with them. Staring at the figure of the old man in the garden, he said in a worried tone, 'I wish I could be sure of him, Dan. I wish he was a dumb, stupid man who wouldn't know or care whether you were worth anything . . . Well, come on.' He opened the gate bravely, but he felt shy and unimportant.

'Hello, son. What's on your mind?' Mr Kemp called from the lawn. He was a thin, wiry man in a cream-coloured shirt. He had a grey, untidy moustache, his skin was wrinkled and leathery, but his eyes were always friendly and amused.

'Could I speak to you, Mr Kemp?' Luke asked.

'Of course.'

'It's about Dan. He's a great dog, but I expect you know that as well as I do. I was wondering if you could keep him here for me.'

'Why should I keep Dan here, son?'

'Well, it's like this,' Luke said, fumbling for words awkwardly: 'My uncle won't let me keep him any more . . . says he's too old.' His mouth began to tremble, then he blurted out the story.

'I see, I see,' Mr Kemp said slowly, and he got up and began to stroke the collie's head. 'Of course, Dan's an old dog, son,' he said quietly. 'And sooner or later you've got to get rid of an old dog. Your uncle knows that. Perhaps it's true that Dan isn't worth his keep.'

'He doesn't eat much, Mr Kemp. Just one meal a day.'

'I wouldn't want you to think your uncle was cruel and unfeeling, Luke,' Mr Kemp went on. 'He's a fine man . . . perhaps just a little bit too practical and straightforward.'

'I suppose that's it,' Luke agreed, but he was really waiting and trusting the expression in the old man's eyes.

'Perhaps you should make him a practical proposition.'

'I—I don't know what you mean.'

'Well, beginning with the way you get the cows for me in the evenings,' Mr Kemp said, smiling to himself. 'In fact, I don't think you need me to go along with you at all. Now, supposing I gave you half a crown a week. Would you get the cows in for me every night?'

'Of course I would, Mr Kemp. I like doing it, anyway.'

'All right, son. It's a deal. Now I'll tell you what to do. Go back to your uncle, and before he has a chance to open up on you, you say right out that you've come to him with a business proposition. Say it like a man, just like that. Offer to pay him the half a crown a week for the dog's keep.'

'But my uncle doesn't need half a crown, Mr Kemp,' Luke said uneasily.

'Of course not,' Mr Kemp agreed. 'It's the principle of the thing. Be confident. Remember that he's got nothing against the dog. Go on, son. Let me know how you do,' he added, with an amused smile. 'If I know your uncle at all, I think it'll work.'

'I'll try it, Mr Kemp,' Luke said. 'Thanks very much.' But he didn't have any confidence, for even though he knew that Mr Kemp was a wise old man who would not deceive him, he couldn't believe that half a crown a week would stop his uncle, who was an important man. 'Come on, Dan,' he called, and he went slowly and apprehensively back to the house.

When they were going up the path, his aunt cried from the open window, 'Henry, Henry, in heaven's name, it's Luke with Dan!'

Ten paces from the verandah, Luke stopped and waited nervously for his uncle to come out. Uncle Henry came out in a rush, but when he saw the collie and Luke standing there, he stopped stiffly, turned pale and his mouth hung open loosely.

'Luke,' he whispered, 'that dog had a stone round his neck.'

'I fished him out of the stream,' Luke said uneasily.

'Oh. Oh, I see,' Uncle Henry said, and gradually the colour came back to his face. 'You fished him out, eh?' he asked, still looking at the dog uneasily. 'Well, you shouldn't have done that. I told Sam Carter to get rid of the dog, you know.'

'Just a minute, Uncle Henry,' Luke said, trying not to falter.

He gained confidence as Aunt Helen came out and stood beside her husband, for her eyes seemed to be gentle, and he went on bravely, 'I want to make you a practical proposition, Uncle Henry.'

'A what?' Uncle Henry asked, still feeling insecure, and wishing the boy and the dog weren't confronting him.

'A practical proposition,' Luke blurted out quickly. 'I know Dan isn't worth his keep to you. I don't suppose he's worth anything to anybody but me. So I'll pay you half a crown a week for his keep.'

'What's this?' Uncle Henry asked, looking bewildered. 'Where would you get half a crown a week, Luke?'

'I'm going to get the cows in every night for Mr Kemp.'

'Oh, for heaven's sake, Henry,' Aunt Helen pleaded, looking distressed, 'let him keep the dog!' and she fled into the house.

'None of that kind of talk!' Uncle Henry called after her. 'We've got to be sensible about this!' But he was shaken himself, and overwhelmed with a distress that destroyed all his confidence. As he sat down slowly in the rocking chair and stroked the side of his big face, he wanted to say weakly, 'All right, keep the dog,' but he was ashamed of being so weak and sentimental. He stubbornly refused to yield to this emotion; he was trying desperately to turn his emotion into a bit of good useful commonsense, so he could justify his distress. So he rocked and pondered.

At last he smiled. 'You're a smart young fellow, Luke,' he said slowly. 'Imagine you working it out like this. I'm tempted to accept your proposition.'

'Oh, thanks, Uncle Henry.'

'I'm accepting it because I think you'll learn something out of this,' he went on ponderously. 'You'll learn that useless luxuries cost the smartest of men hard-earned money.'

'I don't mind.'

'Well, it's a thing you'll have to learn sometime. I think you'll learn, too, because you certainly seem to have a practical streak in you. It's a streak I like to see in a boy. All right, son,' he said, and he smiled with relief and went into the house.

Turning to Dan, Luke whispered softly, 'Well, what do you know about that?'

As he sat down on the step with the collie beside him and listened to Uncle Henry talking to his wife, he began to glow with exultation. Then gradually his exultation began to change to a vast wonder that Mr Kemp should have had such a perfect understanding of Uncle Henry. He began to dream of someday being as wise as old Mr Kemp and knowing exactly how to handle people. It was possible, too, that he had already learned some of the things about his uncle that his father had wanted him to learn.

Putting his head down on the dog's neck, he vowed to himself fervently that he would always have some money on hand, no matter what became of him, so that he would be able to protect all that was truly valuable from the practical people in the world.

Jenny *by Emma Langland*

Until last week, Paula had never really noticed Jenny Hetherington, and that was strange because they'd been at school together for nearly six years—ever since Infants. She knew what Jenny looked like of course, black hair in pigtails, darker skinned than the rest, a bit ugly really—but she'd never talked to her or played with her, and neither had anyone else.

The only time Jenny had made herself in any way conspicuous was hardly of her own doing. She had an attack of asthma in Morning Assembly. It was quite an event. Mr Penn stopped in the middle of a prayer and asked one of the teachers to take her out for a drink of water, and Jenny was led away wheezing as if each breath was her last. But no-one felt particularly sorry for her, no-one asked after her when she came into the classroom later on—to them it was just a spectacle, something different. Morning Assembly was always more fun if someone was sick, or fainted, or if Mr Penn read out the wrong hymn number and had to be corrected by Miss Leach at the piano.

Normally Jenny faded into her surroundings wherever she was: the teachers never paid her any attention because they never had any cause to. She worked away quietly by herself, never put her hand up, never messed about. In plays, she was always the one who pulled the curtains: when they had to find a partner to work with, she often seemed to get left out. She had no friends and didn't seem to want any.

Back in Infants, none of this seemed to matter at all—they just left her alone and she left them alone. But it began to matter later on, not much, but a bit. People started calling her 'Jenny Gippo'—Paula thought it must be because of her black hair: and there was some teasing, but no more than her fair share. One of her gymshoes would 'disappear' just before the PE lesson, or Gary would come up behind her and pull her pigtails. But they all had nicknames, their shoes were always 'disappearing' and Gary was always pulling everyone's hair.

The trouble started when Jenny developed the habit of staring. At first Paula paid no attention, she knew there was paint on her face and she did have a sty under her left eye. But her sty disappeared after a few days, and she'd made quite sure her face was clean. Jenny still went on staring at her. Every time she looked up from her book, she found Jenny staring straight at her as if she were a thing and not a person at all. Paula was beginning to feel unnerved by it, so she decided not to look at Jenny unless she had to.

She had forgotten all about it until she heard Gary going on about it last Friday afternoon in playtime. 'I'll do her if I catch her at it again. I'll do her.' He was glaring across the playground at Jenny who was picking cement out of the high brick wall by the road.

'What's she done?' Paula asked.

'Gawpin'. Staring—that's what. I've only got to look at her, just look that's all, and she's gawpin' back at me.'

'She can't be,' Rosemary said from behind him. 'She can't be all the time.'

'What d'you mean, she can't be?' Gary turned on her. 'I ought to know, oughtn't I? I ought to know when someone's staring at me. It's like Muhammad Ali before a fight. All morning she's been at it—like a zombie she is.'

'Well, it can't be all morning, not all morning,' Rosemary insisted. 'Because she was staring at me too, as if I had two heads or something. And that was all morning too—every time I looked up. So she couldn't have . . .'

'And me,' Paula interrupted. 'And me too. She was doing it to me as well you know.'

'I'll do her if she does it again,' Gary repeated. Gary was always 'doing' people—he wasn't much good at anything else, but no-one dared tell him so. After all he was the biggest boy in the school and a bully with a fearsome reputation, so everyone did what Gary said and steered well clear of him.

'I know,' said Rosemary, her voice dropping to a confidential whisper. 'I know—we'll stare her out. Like Muhammad Ali, like you said, Gary.'

'I'll do her,' Gary muttered. He wasn't listening.

'Let's stare her out first,' Paula said. 'And then you can "do" her afterwards—if it doesn't work, that is.'

It was last lesson, and there was a television programme on the Vikings that Mrs Fishwick made them watch every week. Fishiwick was obsessed with the wretched Vikings; for her the programme was the highlight of the week. She'd read them all the legends—they knew more about Baldor and Thor and Wodin than they did about Robin Hood. She'd covered the walls with great pictures of Viking Longships filled with long-haired blond warriors. No that's wrong, not 'warriors'. They weren't allowed to call them 'warriors'. Mrs Fishwick said they were peace-loving farmers with a desire to travel the world. That took most of the fun out of it—they were bored silly with Vikings.

The blinds were down and the classroom darkened for the programme. It was all about Leif Ericson, Leif the Lucky. Paula was fed up in five minutes, she knew all about him already. Then she remembered Jenny and looked across at her table on the far side of the classroom. Jenny was staring back, straight at her. She could see the white, shimmering light of the television glinting on Jenny's eyes. She was just about to look away when she remembered what Rosemary had said out in the playground, what they'd all agreed to do—stare her out. Paula sat back in her chair, folded her arms and stared back across the room. Nothing was going to make her look away first.

It was easy enough to start with. Paula was able to forget who was behind the white eyes that gazed steadily back at her. The rest of the face could have been anybody's, the eyes were all she could see. The television sounded hollow in the classroom, not at all like the one at home. Someone was droning on about Leif the Lucky—did he get to America or didn't he? Paula didn't much care one way or the other. Then she began thinking what a good idea it was to name people like that, like Leif the Lucky, Eric the Red; and she was thinking of a name for anyone who came to mind—'Fishiwick the Fuzzy' (on account of her hair), 'Gary the Ghastly', 'Jenny the Gippo' . . . Jenny. Paula was still staring into those eyes. She felt a bit sleepy and her eyes were pricking with concentration. She wanted the chance to blink just once, then she could start again. She opened her eyes wider and forced herself to look just to one side of Jenny's eyes. There was something in Jenny's eyes she wanted to avoid—perhaps if she looked just a little to one side, perhaps she could still win. She tried it, but immediately found herself being drawn involuntarily back into the full beam of Jenny's gaze. She pulled her chair in, propped her chin on her forearms and glared back. She would not be beaten.

The lights were on and Mrs Fishwick was shouting her name. 'Paula! Paula! I will not have children going off to sleep in my class. Do you hear me, Paula?' She was wide awake by now. 'It's always the same these days—too much television the night before. Heaven only knows what you find to watch.' She paused. 'And you're not the only one Paula. Gary, Rosemary, stand up.'

Gary's face was puffy and red on one side and Rosemary was blinking at the light. Mrs Fishwick was going on. 'I don't know what's the matter with you three. It was an excellent programme—Leif Ericson is one of the most exciting figures in Viking history—and you drop off to sleep.'

'We seen it before, Miss,' Gary said. He was always answering back, and he knew that if there was one thing that made Fishiwick mad it was calling her 'Miss'.

'No you have not, Gary Hibben,' she stormed, 'And don't you dare talk to me like that . . . after the way you've behaved.'

She was red in the face now and Paula knew there would have to be a punishment. If only Gary had kept his big mouth shut—just this once. 'Very well. You will all three write me two full sides on the voyages of Leif Ericson, and I want it before the end of school on Monday. Do you understand me?' Paula was right. 'Either that, or it'll be Mr Penn's office—and none of you want that, do you?' No-one did, particularly Gary. The last time he'd been sent in there for cheeking Mrs Fishwick, he'd emerged ten minutes later with his eyes red from crying.

Paula picked up her anorak from the cloakroom and waited outside for Gary and Rosemary. Jenny walked past her, shrugging herself into her coat: there was a faraway look on her face, as if she were living in another world. It was that look that made Paula begin to wonder. Something strange had happened in the classroom: all three of them had tried to stare Jenny out, all three of them had fallen asleep. It could hardly be just a coincidence.

Rosemary came out. 'I tried,' Paula said. 'I really tried, but she wouldn't stop looking.'

'I don't understand it,' Rosemary said. 'She can't be looking at three places at once, can she? She can't be looking at you, me and Gary all at the same time, can she?'

'Perhaps Gary forgot,' Paula said. 'Perhaps it was just you and me.'

'He can't have. He was asleep, wasn't he? Just like us. She made us go to sleep, I know she did.'

'That's hypnotism,' Paula said.

'What's that mean?'

'It's when a doctor or a witch or someone like that sends you to sleep. They talk to you quietly and dangle a watch in front of your face.'

'But Jenny wasn't dangling . . .' Rosemary stopped short. There were angry shouts from the other end of the playground. They both knew who it was—there was only one boy who bellowed like that. They turned the corner to see a small crowd over by the brick wall.

Gary was standing head and shoulders above everyone else, and through the legs of the crowd they could see that there was someone lying on the ground. They barged through the crowd to get a better look. Gary was breathing heavily, his fists still held up to his chest and clenched hard. Jenny was lying on the ground with her coat torn off at the buttons, and there was blood running down her chin from her nose and falling onto her white blouse. No one was saying anything, they just gaped in stunned silence, and Jenny's face registered nothing, no pain, no anger, no fear, nothing. You could see Gary had been crying, and that seemed strange because there wasn't a scratch on him: he was standing there ready for more, and she was lying flat on her back against the wall with blood streaming from her nose.

Gary lowered his fists slowly, looked as if he was about to say something and thought better of it. He pushed his way past and began running. Jenny was getting to her feet, brushing the blood away from her chin so that it smeared upwards towards her eye. She was watching Gary as he ran out of the school gates and disappeared across the road, and then she said in a quiet deliberate voice as expressionless as her face: 'I'll kill you.'

Mrs Fishwick was at the main door, clapping her hands at them. 'Off home with you—you know you're not supposed to play around in the school grounds after school hours. Now go on, off you go, and mind that main road.'

On Sunday, Rosemary came round to Paula's house as usual, and they spent all the afternoon up in Paula's bedroom trying to hypnotize each other, first by gazing long and deep into each other's eyes, and then by following the swing of a conker on the end of a piece of string, to and fro, to and fro. It was all a complete waste of time, neither of them felt at all sleepy.

'I give up,' Rosemary said, throwing the conker into the corner of the room. 'We can't do it, and even if we could, it still wouldn't explain how she could be staring at all three of us at the same time. It's impossible.'

'Nothing's impossible,' Paula said. 'Not for some people.'

'What do you mean?'

'You know, witches and things like that: nothing's impossible for them,' Paula said, thinking aloud.

'No such thing as witches,' Rosemary said, 'That's all in books—load of rubbish.'

'Anyway,' said Paula. 'Some people are different. They've got powers to work miracles and things . . .'

'Like Jesus, I suppose,' Rosemary scoffed. 'I bet he didn't go around staring at people and putting them to sleep.'

'You can have bad miracles as well as good ones,' Paula said. 'Perhaps she put a curse on us, you never know.'

'Paula!' Rosemary sat up suddenly. 'That's it! That's it!'

'What is?'

'Jenny. Jenny Gippo. She's a gypsy, she's a real gypsy. They can put a curse on you, can't they?' Rosemary was right. That would account for everything. Paula felt a shiver creeping up her spine and she found she had to swallow hard.

'But all we did was stare at her,' Paula said. 'That's all, isn't it? It was Gary who thumped her, not us. We never touched her, did we?'

'She wouldn't put a curse on us just for looking at her, would she?' Rosemary had gone quite pale.

'She was doing it first,' said Paula. 'She started it. Wasn't our fault.'

Rosemary was on her feet now. 'Oh Paula, you don't think she really meant it, do you?'

'Meant what?'

'All that about killing Gary. She said she'd kill him, remember?'

' 'Course she won't,' Paula said quietly. 'That was just talk, that's all. She was just saying it.' But Paula was remembering Jenny's voice in the playground. That wasn't just talk and she knew it. If Jenny could put all three of them to sleep at once, it couldn't be too difficult for her to do away with Gary.

Neither of them ate anything for tea, and they never mentioned Jenny after that. It was too serious a subject to discuss, it was too threatening for both of them. They looked at the television without watching it, and when it was time to go they promised each other they'd stick together at school the next day—just in case.

At Assembly on Monday morning there was a strange man on the platform next to Mr Penn. He didn't seem to know any of the hymns or prayers. He just stood there looking down over the rows of children and blowing his nose from time to time. He was one of those people who spring-clean their noses after every blow. Then Mr Penn kept making mistakes in the prayers. Everyone knew he was nervous in Assembly—you could see the prayer book shaking up and down in his hand, but he never made mistakes, not Mr Penn. Paula knew something was up and looked across to Rosemary who frowned back at her, tossing her head towards Gary's place by the radiator. Paula leaned forward. Gary's chair was empty, he wasn't there. She checked all around the hall, but he was nowhere. She felt Rosemary looking hard at her, and she didn't dare look back, she knew they were thinking the same thing. Jenny had done it, she must have done it. They looked over to Jenny's place. She was there, praying with her eyes tight shut.

Mr Penn was waving at them to sit down, and everyone was much quicker about settling down than usual.

'Good morning, children,' Mr Penn announced, straightening his tie as he always did. The chorus came back at him: 'Good morning, Mister Penn', it was more like a dirge than a greeting. 'Now, children, this is Chief Inspector Bridges from the Police Station. I want you all to listen very carefully to what he has to say. It's very important.' And Mr Penn stepped back carefully, sat down and crossed his legs.

The Police Inspector cleared his throat noisily and shuffled forward to the front of the platform. 'Can you hear me at the back?' he boomed out. No-one bothered to answer, no-one that is except for little Katie Doyle from the Infants who was sitting right under his feet. 'Yes,' she squeaked. Everyone laughed except Paula and Rosemary. They all hushed again.

'It's about Gary Hibben,' said the Inspector slowly. Paula felt her skin tingling all over her body. Jenny had done it, she really had gone and done it. 'Gary Hibben,' he repeated. 'Now you all know Gary, don't you?'

'Yes,' piped Katie again. No-one laughed this time.

'Well, Gary left school on Friday afternoon last, just like the rest of you, but he never went home—we don't know where he is.' He paused and cleared his throat again. 'Now I've no doubt that we'll find him soon enough, but we can't do it without your help. Now, I want you all to think hard, try hard to remember. Last Friday afternoon, the last afternoon you were at school, did anyone see Gary after he left school on Friday? Did one of you walk some of the way home with him? Did you see him with anyone else—a grownup maybe? Perhaps one of you stopped off with him somewhere, to buy some sweets maybe? Or the canal? The park then? Now, are you all thinking?' Paula and Rosemary did not have to think, they knew already. 'You know, Gary's Mum and Dad are very worried, they want him back and I expect you do too. So, if any one of you remembers any little thing, you must tell me, right?'

Mr Penn stood up again, and waited for the muttering and the shuffles to die down before he spoke. 'The Inspector will want to ask each of you in turn. We'll start with the Infants and work up through the school, and when your turn comes, come to the office. And don't worry, it won't be nearly as painful as the 'flu injections.' Mr Penn's little jokes never really came off.

It was bad enough for the others, but for Paula and Rosemary work was impossible that morning. They tried not to look at Jenny and yet every now and then they found themselves peering across at her from behind their books, searching her face for any tell-tale sign of the guilt she must be feeling. But neither of them dared look for long enough in case Jenny turned suddenly and caught them at it; however, for Paula it was long enough to decide that Jenny really was a gypsy, she had to be with hair like that.

Rosemary seemed on the verge of tears by now, and so Paula tried to forget her and to concentrate on her work. Mrs Fishwick was prowling round all the time, checking sums and marking their English; but there was very little to mark, all of them were waiting to be called to the office to meet the Police Inspector. By first playtime, Mrs Fishwick had given up trying to make them work, and had resorted to a story. No-one had been called to the office. In an hour and a quarter Paula had done two sums and got both of them wrong, but she had decided that she would tell the Inspector everything.

She caught up with Rosemary by the drinking-fountain. 'I'm going to tell him,' she said. 'About the fight and what she said, and about her being a gypsy and everything. I'm going to tell him.' But Rosemary wasn't listening, she was gaping at the school gates and her mouth had dropped open as if she had seen a ghost. 'It's him,' she whispered. 'It's him.'

Gary was strolling in through the gate, a bag slung over his shoulder, and he was whistling ostentatiously. No-one else had seen him yet. They ran over to him and pulled him in behind the lavatory wall.

'Where've you been?' Rosemary was shaking him and there were tears pouring down her face.

'What happened?' Paula said. 'What did she do to you?'

'Happened? What did she do? What did who do? What you on about? Here let me go.' Gary pulled himself free.

'The police are here—they're looking for you.' Rosemary was calmer now.

'Police? The cops here? After me?' Gary sounded worried. 'What for? I done nothing wrong.'

'You never went home,' Rosemary said, pulling at him again. 'What happened?'

'Let go of me, will you.' He appeared to be thinking. 'Did Dad tell them then?'

'He said you never went home,' Paula said.

'We thought . . .' Rosemary stopped herself.

'I've been up the football at Leeds, that's all. They can't get me for that, can they?'

'You should have told someone,' Paula said, forgetting who she was talking to.

'I couldn't, could I?' Gary said picking at his hand. 'Me dad said I mustn't go to football, not after all that trouble at Manchester. Said I wasn't old enough.' Gary was crying, you could hear it in his voice. 'I went anyway. I had to, everyone else was. And I can't go home, he'll do me, I know he will,' Gary sniffed, wiping his nose with the back of his hand.

Paula and Rosemary stayed in that afternoon to finish their writing on Leif the Lucky. Gary never bothered. He was too busy showing off in the playground; everyone wanted to bask in the reflected glory of big Gary Hibben who had been on the run from the police. And anyway, Fishiwick never even asked for the writing, she must have forgotten all about it.

They're still not sure about Jenny.

The Quarry *by Alan Paton*

Everywhere the city was driving back nature, to the South and the West and the North. Only the East was safe, for there lay the ocean. Skyscrapers stood on the places where elephants had crashed through the forest. Hippopotamus Pool was a city square full of the smells of buses; Lions' River ran down a straight concrete channel into the Bay.

Only Mitchell's Quarry had resisted the march of the city. It was a stony scar cut out of the side of Pigeon Hill, and though it was ugly it was a piece of nature. The large green pigeons had long since gone, but small birds and animals still clung to it, and lived in the trees and grass that ran down each side of the scar. Frogs and very small fish lived in the pools. Children were attracted there, for it was the only bit of wildness in the city.

It was Johnny Day's favourite place. Sometimes he sat by the pools for hours, watching the fish. Sometimes he climbed up through the trees and sat on the very edge of the quarry, in the cool exciting wind from the dancing ocean. He more than once wondered whether anyone could climb down, but Tom Hesketh, who was sixteen and very manly, told him that it was impossible and had never been done, and never would be done unless one came down on a rope. One could climb up from the bottom and Tom had done it once with two of his friends.

'Which way did you take, Tom?'

'I'm not telling you,' said Tom, 'it's not for kids. Can't you see the notice?'

The notice said, NO CLIMBING, BY ORDER, only whose order it was, no-one knew.

'And I'm not doing it again,' said Tom, 'because when I was halfway up, all I wanted to do was to come down again, and I couldn't.'

Sitting by one of the pools, Johnny looked at the quarry face, wondering which way Tom had taken. All he knew was that Tom had begun by the notice board, saying NO CLIMBING, BY ORDER, and that is where he would begin too, on the day after Christmas Day. He would climb in a direction half right where it seemed there was a track of footholds made for just such a purpose. Halfway up the quarry face the track seemed to peter out, but another track bearing half-left could be seen some feet higher. All that he must do was to find the way from one to the other.

On the morning of the day after Christmas Day Johnny arrived at the quarry and found nobody there. Confident of success he took off his jacket and cap, and laid them on a stone under the notice board. He was wearing sandshoes, because that was what Tom Hesketh had worn. He looked up at the quarry face which was roughly a perpendicular plane. He placed his right foot in a niche that seemed to have been made for it. He drew his left foot up and now stood about a foot above the level floor and the pools. The climb had begun, and the feeling of the climber was not nervousness but pure ambition, strong in one so young, for he was only eleven.

It certainly seemed that the track had been cut deliberately, perhaps to enable the quarry workers to climb the face. There was always a place for the foot, and the rock face inclined away from him, a few degrees from the perpendicular, so that he had a feeling of security. There was no need so far for skill or ingenuity, for the method was simple—a hold with the hands, right foot up, left foot up, an inching forward on the same small ledge if possible, a searching for another hold with the hands and another small ledge for the right foot. He was about twenty feet up, and could see that he could return safely if it was necessary. He looked down, and this gave him a feeling of exhilaration. He looked up, but decided not to do it again, because it seemed to reveal his own insignificance against the vast wall of the quarry, and above that the vast emptiness of the sky. From now on he would confine his attention to the handhold, the foothold and the rock face that so obligingly allowed him to lean against it.

The track continued as before for a short distance and he was at a height of about thirty feet when he reached a place where the rock face became suddenly perpendicular for a length of some three feet, so that he would not be able to lean against it. He wondered if he could take a step direct from safety to safety, but knew that the step would be too big for him. His only hope was a good hold for hands and feet. He was the slightest bit nervous, because he knew something else too, that if he decided to take the next two steps it would be twice as hard to return.

Tom Hesketh had said to him, 'If you're frightened to take the next step, don't take it, just climb down, if you can. If you can't climb down, then you've just got to take the next step, that's all. And I tell you, kid, it's dangerous getting frightened up there.'

Well he might be a bit nervous but he wasn't climbing down. He could see the trail clearly, and it looked easy except for this one next step. There was a place for the hands and a place for the right foot, just as good as any he had used so far.

Someone shouted at him from below. It was a big Indian man who was shouting with some Indian boys.

'Come down, sonny,' shouted the big Indian man.

Johnny shook his head. Without looking he pointed at the sky.

The big Indian man shook his head too.

'No, no,' he shouted. 'It's too dangerous, sonny. Come down.'

Again Johnny shook his head, and pointed up. The Indian man tried warnings.

'Last year,' he shouted, 'an Indian boy was killed here. He was climbing the same way you are climbing now.' This wasn't true. There never had been such an Indian boy, but the Indian man believed that if the end was good, one shouldn't worry too much about the means. When the warnings failed, he invoked divine aid.

'God sent me here,' he shouted. 'to tell you to come down. He is telling you now to come down. He does not mean for you to be up there. If you don't come down, He will be plenty angry.' He added a clever afterthought. 'Just like He was angry with that Indian boy.'

'Don't let anything take your mind off your hands and feet,' said Tom, 'or off the rock face. Don't think of the height, or of the spectators. Don't look at birds or ships on the sea. Just think of the climb.'

That is what Johnny did. To the despair of the big Indian man, and the admiration of the Indian boys, he addressed himself to the task of finding a place for his right hand and a place for his right foot, and when he had found them, he took the dangerous step. It was done. The ledge was generous, and he brought up his left foot. Tom's instruction was immediately forgotten, and he looked down at the growing crowd of Indian men and women and boys and girls, and African men from the factory near the quarry.

The big Indian man shouted at him again to come down, and it was this very shouting that brought Tom's instruction back to Johnny's mind, so that the louder and more desperate the warnings and the threats, the less he paid attention to them. He took his next step with confidence, and the trail before him was now straightforward and easy for at least seven steps. Then it stopped dead. He braced himself to look up, and there, about ten or twelve feet above him, he could see the second trail that ran half-left, and would take him to the top. He could see almost at once that he could go no further in a half-right direction, that he would have to climb straight up. He could also see toeholds for the first five feet, for that was his own height. It would all depend whether there were handholds also; that he would have to tell by feeling for them, partly because he was apprehensive about looking up, and partly because the rock face seemed to be nearer the perpendicular when one thought of climbing it perpendicularly.

These thoughts and speculations took him some minutes, so that the crowd below knew that he was facing some kind of crisis. He was nearly fifty feet up, about one-third of the height of the quarry face. There were now a hundred people watching him, talking to each other, but not loudly, because they were subdued by contemplation of the dangers that lay ahead. The boys were filled with admiration and awe, and the women with tender feeling and care. It was a white boy, it is true, but there in the danger and excitement of his journey up the quarry face, he had become one of their own. The boys wished him luck and the women shook their heads, unable to be indifferent to either his naughtiness or his plight.

Johnny lifted his right foot to make the first step of the ascent, and this action put the big Indian man into a panic.

'Sonny,' he cried, 'true's God, don't go up any more. You'll die, sonny, and no-one here wants you to die. Sonny, I ask you to come down.' He went down on his knees on the quarry floor, and said, 'I pray God to make you come down. I pray God not to be angry with you.' The women there, both Indian and African, seeing him kneeling there, cried out 'shame', but not because they thought his action was shameful, they were merely saying how sad the whole thing was.

The Indian man was now struck by a new idea, and he shouted, 'Sonny, what's your address?' Johnny heard him but he tried to pay no attention, needing it all for the dangerous piece ahead. However, the question disturbed him slightly, and he brought his right foot down again, causing the crowd to give a composite groan, with many meanings. The Indian man took it as a reprieve, and shouted, 'Sonny, I pray to God, give me your address.'

It was now clear to all but his would-be rescuer that the small boy intended to continue the climb. His small exploratory movements showed that he meant to go up, not down. Again he placed his right foot, but this time he pulled himself up, causing the Indian man to rise from his knees and to collapse groaning onto a rock with his hands covering his eyes. So was silenced his vocal opposition to the climb, but the rest were quiet too, speaking in low voices, even whispers, as Johnny placed his hands and his foot, and pulled himself up, two feet now above the safety of the sloping trail. Then again the hands exploring, the right foot testing, the body bracing, the small boy like a fly on a cinema screen, except that he was no intruder, rather the creator of a drama never before witnessed in this city, of a crowd of every colour and class and tongue, bound all of them together for these moments by unbreakable bonds, to a small white boy climbing a quarry face made of a stone that knew nothing of admiration or anxiety or pity. And again a step, and again the low talking, and again the exploring hands and the testing foot, and again the bracing of the body. And down below silence, and silent prayers, and silent apprehension. The Indian man took his hands from his eyes and watched despairingly; it was clear he was in an agony of care and pity over this child of an alien race, many of whose members had shown neither care nor pity for himself or his people.

And up above again the winning of another step, again the murmur from below, from a crowd growing every moment, swollen by people streaming over the waste ground between the quarry and the tarred road. There they stood, shoulder to shoulder, ruler and ruled, richer and poorer, white and black and yellow and brown, with their eyes fixed on a small piece of whiteness halfway up the quarry face, and those of them who knew a thing or two, knew that the boy was in a position of considerable danger.

Fortunately Johnny himself did not know it. He was surprised that his right hand searching above his head had found another generous ledge, at least nine inches wide. Once he had reached it, he would be able to rest, even perhaps to look upward to plan the last piece of climbing that would enable him to reach the half-left trail. Therefore he set out to reach it, alternately terrifying and gratifying the watching crowd below.

The crowd did not realize the achievement when at last Johnny's feet were both planted on the nine-inch ledge. He himself decided not only to rest, but to allow his attention to be diverted from the climb. The ledge was so wide that he could turn himself about for the first time, stand with his back to the quarry face, and look down on the hundreds of people below. Some of them clapped and cheered him, some of them looked at him out of troubled eyes. The big Indian man stood up from the rock onto which he had collapsed, and called out, in a less assured voice than hitherto, for the small boy to come down, but after another man had spoken quietly to him, he desisted, and it was generally understood that the second man had told him that the small boy had reached a point of no return, and it was better to leave him alone, and to pray rather for his salvation.

For three minutes, four minutes, it must have been, Johnny stood with his back to the quarry face. After acknowledging the crowd's cheers, he had cut them off from attention, and stood there reassembling his small boy's powers. Everything was silent when again he turned his face to the quarry wall. The foothold was there, the handhold for the left hand was there, but of the handhold for the right hand there was no sign whatsoever. At first he could not believe it, but when he tried again he knew there was no doubt of it. Had the handhold been perpendicularly above the toehold he might have done it, but it was at least a foot to the left of his body line. No-one could pull himself up from such a position.

A growl went up from the crowd, of defeat and frustration, and from the more knowledgeable, of sharpened anxiety. Again the questing hands, again the finding of nothing. The small boy, leaving his two arms in this upstretched position, put his face to the face of the quarry, almost as if he were weeping or praying, which indeed is what some thought he was doing. He brought down his arms and caused the crowd to groan and shudder as his left foot explored the rock below him, trying to find the foothold he had used to reach the ledge.

In complete silence they watched him put his foot on it, but after a moment he withdrew and again laid his face against the face of the quarry. It was then clear that his ambition to climb had gone, and in its place was the frightenedness of a small boy. Again he turned himself round so that he faced the crowd, who could see clearly his loneliness and despair. His movements, so splendidly co-ordinated until now, gave alarming signs of randomness, and for one terrible moment it seemed that he might panic and fall.

This was the signal for a young African man of about twenty to take charge.

'Hi, sonny,' he shouted, waving with outstretched arm to the boy, 'don't be frightened. Thomas Ndhlovu is coming.'

On his way to the starting-point by the notice board, Thomas spoke to a white man who seemed to be senior to the others.

'Get the police, master, or the fire brigade. I go up to stay with the small boy.'

Then he started his climb amid a new noise of laughs, cheers, approval and advice. Thomas soon showed himself to be vigorous and unskilled, and his friends below, who had been so anxious about the first climber, made jokes about the second. As for Thomas himself, whenever he had brought off what he thought a piece of good climbing, he would turn to the crowd and raise his clenched fist, to be greeted by cheers and laughter. Every few steps he would shout at the small boy, urging him to be of good heart, because one Thomas Ndhlovu was coming. The small boy himself had recovered from his panic and watched absorbedly the progress of his saviour. What had been a tense and terrifying affair had become a kind of festival. Jests and laughter had replaced groans and sighs, and Thomas, with intention somewhat foolish, climbed flamboyantly and wildly, shouting encouragement in English to the small boy and exchanging banter in Zulu with his friends on the ground. It was only when he reached the end of the first trail, and began to inspect the sharp perpendicular ascent, that the crowd again fell silent.

Thomas however would not tolerate this new respect. Turning round he shouted something at his friends that caused much laughter. He too made the exploratory motions of hands and it was very clear that he was caricaturing the small boy's motions. Nevertheless the laughter died away as he began the ascent and the atmosphere was tense, without being fearful. When at last he placed his foot on the nine-inch ledge, rulers and ruled, richer and poorer, joined in an ovation of shouting and clapping, which was doubled and redoubled when he too turned to face the crowd. He smiled down at the small white boy and put his hand on his shoulder, as if to assure him that no-one fell from a ledge when Thomas Ndhlovu was on it.

'Now be quiet,' he said, 'some time the police come, and the fire brigade, and you go home to your mother.'

The small boy said, 'Thanks a million,' and Thomas said, 'What your mother say?'

'I won't tell my mother,' said Johnny.

Thomas laughed uproariously and pointed at the crowd below, where newspaper men were taking photographs and interviewing spectators.

'Tomorrow,' said Thomas, 'big picture in paper, you and me. Your mother open paper, she say, what you doing there with that native boy?'

He thought this very funny, and for a time occupied himself with it. Then he asked, 'What's your name, sonny?'

'Johnny Day.'

'Johnny Day, eh? Very good name. My name Thomas Ndhlovu.'

'Very good name too,' said Johnny.

'Police coming,' said Thomas pointing. 'When police coming other times, Thomas running. Now police coming, Thomas staying.'

The arrival of the police was greeted with great good humour, for here was an occasion on which their arrival was welcome. Words in Zulu were shouted at them, compliments tinged with satire, for the crowd was feeling happy and free. The policemen grasped the whole situation immediately. Two of them, armed with ropes, set off up through the trees that grew at the side of the quarry and in a few minutes had reached the upper edge, where they took up a position directly above the man and the boy. Instructions were shouted and a rope was lowered to Thomas, who, once he had the cradle-like end in his hand, laughed with uproarious delight. To the end of this rope was attached another which Thomas threw to the policemen below. More instructions were shouted and Thomas soon had the small boy in the cradle. The policemen above lowered the cradle down the quarry wall. The policemen below held it away from the stony face. In one minute Johnny was on the quarry floor, lost to sight in a swirling multi-coloured mass, shouting their joy and congratulation.

This celebration was still in progress as Thomas Ndhlovu landed on the quarry floor, when it transferred itself to him. Everybody, white, yellow, brown, black, wanted to shake hands with him, to thank him for his splendid act, to ask God to bless him. The Indian man, now fully restored, was one of the most enthusiastic of these participators.

'Come, sonny,' said the senior white man. 'Tell me where you live and I'll take you home.'

'I must thank Thomas first,' said Johnny.

The senior white man looked at the tumultuous scene. 'How are you going to do that?' he said.

'I'll wait,' said Johnny.

But he did not need to wait. The policemen cleared a way through the mob of congratulators, and there, under the eyes of authority, Johnny Day put out his hand and thanked Thomas Ndhlovu again for the act which, for all we know, saved his life. This second evidence of gratitude was extremely pleasurable to Thomas, and moved to great heights by it, he led the small white boy to the notice board which said, NO CLIMBING, BY ORDER. What he said, no-one heard, for it was lost in an outburst of catcalls, laughter, jeering, and cheering.

The Goalkeeper's Revenge

by Bill Naughton

Sim Dalt had two long, loose arms, spindly legs, a bony face with gleaming brown eyes, and, from the age of twelve, was reckoned to be a bit touched in the head.

Goalkeeping was the main interest in Sim's life. In his nursery days the one indoor pastime that satisfied him was when his mother kicked a rubber ball from the living-room into the kitchen, while Sim stood goal at the middle door. It was rare even then that he let one pass.

He later attended Scuttle Street elementary school, where he was always gnawed with the ferocious wish for four o'clock, when he could dash to the cinder park to play goalie for some team or other. Even in the hot summer days, Sim would cajole a few non-players into a game of football. 'Shoot 'em in, chaps,' he would yell, after lovingly arranging the heaps of jackets for the goalposts, 'the harder the better.'

At twelve he was picked as goalkeeper for his school team. 'If you let any easy 'uns through,' the captain, Bob Thropper, threatened him, 'I'll bust your shins in!'

But he had no need to warn Sim, for it was rare indeed that anyone could get a ball past him.

It was near the end of the season, and Scuttle Street were at the top of the league and in the final for the Mayor's Shield, when a new and very thorough inspector visited the school. He found Sim's scholastic ability to be of such a low order that he directed him at once to Clinic Street special school.

'I suppose you could continue to play for us until the end of the season,' said Mr Speckle, at a meeting of the team, 'and then, at least, you'll be sure of a medal.'

'What, sir!' interposed Bob Thropper. 'A *cracky school* lad play for us? Ee, sir, that *would* be out of order!'

'But what shall we do about a goalkeeper?' asked the teacher.

The Goalkeeper's Revenge

'Goalkeepers!' snorted Bob. 'I could buy 'em and sell 'em.'

'What,' asked Sim, staring at Bob, 'what do you mean, "buy 'em an' sell 'em"?'

'I mean that they're ten a penny,' grunted Bob, 'especially daft 'uns.' And having made his point he snapped: 'Off with them togs, mate—we want 'em for our next man.' And Sim sadly removed his boots, stockings and shorts. When it came to the jersey he hesitated, but Bob grabbed at it: 'Buy 'em an' sell 'em,' he growled, 'that's me.'

There was a tear close to Sim's eye. 'I'll never buy you,' he hissed, 'but I might sell you one day.'

In adapting himself to his new life he was quick enough to grasp any advantage it might offer. He organised games in the schoolyard, and for two years enjoyed some hectic if not polished goalkeeping. And at the age of fifteen, when his mother took him round to different factories for work, he simulated idiocy so as not to be taken on.

'Now stop this shinanikin,' his mother scolded him, 'you're no more barmy than I am. And you know it.'

'You shoulda told the school inspector that,' remarked Sim.

Every morning, with the 'normal intelligence' boys gaping enviously at him through the factory windows, Sim would set out for the cinder park bouncing and heading a football along the street.

At the age of nineteen he accepted his first job, since it did not interfere with his way of life; also, it had possibilities. It was at Brunt's Amusement Arcade, where the chief attraction was a 'Beat the Goalie' game. There were goal-posts that appeared to be full size, and a real football, and all comers were invited to try to score. It cost threepence for a try, and anyone who scored received sixpence in return. Sim, of course, got the job of goalkeeper.

Maggie Brunt, the owner, was a wizened, red-eyed woman. 'How's it goin', lad?' she would say, giving sly slaps of apparent goodwill on various parts of the goalkeeper's person. By this cunning form of greeting she had caught out a stream of employees who had been fiddling—having one pocket for Maggie and one for themselves.

She tried it out on Sim, time after time, and never once was there the faintest jingle of metal, until finally she decided that the lad must be simple, if not honest. The fact was that Sim—who did things with singular efficiency when he had to—had constructed a special pocket, copiously insulated with cottonwool, and provided with various sections for different coins. Had Maggie turned him upside-down and shaken him like a pepper-pot she would not have heard the faintest jingle, so expertly was it contrived.

There came a day, after some six thrifty years, when Maggie decided to sell the Arcade—and Sim was able to buy it from her. 'Bless you, lad,' sighed Maggie, 'they say you're gone in the head, but I wish there were more like you.'

'It wouldn't do,' remarked Sim, and not without a touch of regret he removed the cottonwool from his pocket.

Bob Thropper's visit to the Arcade was the start of a remarkably prosperous boom for Sim. Bob was a thickset, dark-joweled footballer by this time, and the idol of the Hummerton crowd. His tremendous kicking power had broken many goal-nets, winded or knocked senseless a number of goalkeepers, and on one occasion, it was said, had actually smashed a crossbar.

One night, just after a cup-tie victory, Bob and his team-mates, merry though not drunk, were passing the Arcade, when one suggested having some sport with Sim.

'Skipper,' whispered Stan Mead, 'you smash one in!'

Stan Mead dived into his pocket for threepence, when Sim called out: 'Like to make it pounds instead of pence?'

The challenge was taken up at once, and in a moment eleven pound notes were flung down, and Sim covered these with as many out of his pocket. Then Bob Thropper drew back, took his short, confident run, and let go one of his famous drives. Sim was up like a flash, and brought it down with stylish assurance.

Then with a casual air he threw the ball back. 'Are you covering the twenty-two quid?' he asked.

The money was covered in two minutes. 'What about waiting till somebody nips off for your football boots?' asked Stan Mead.

Bob shook his head. 'I could lick this loon,' he snorted, 'in my bare feet'—and with that he took a second shot. It was good—but not good enough. Sim leapt and caught it on his chest. Bob's face went darker than ever. 'Fetch my boots,' he hissed at Stan Mead, 'an' I'll smash him to bits.'

A huge crowd swayed the Arcade when Bob Thropper prepared to make the third attempt. The forty-four pounds had been covered, so that there was a pile of pound notes on an orange box, with a brick on top of them. After having his boots tied up, Bob Thropper removed his jacket, took off his collar and tie, and nodded to Stan Mead to place the ball. The crowd went silent as he took the short run, and then kicked.

The ball flashed forward—it went like lightning, a knee-high shot. '*Goal!*' yelled a voice from behind. But a long thin figure whizzed through the air. There was a thud, the figure dropped to the ground. Nobody could be sure what had happened—until Sim stood up. His face was white. But he had the ball clutched against his heart. Slowly he went towards the orange box and picked up the money. 'Closing time!' he whispered in a low, clear voice. The crowd set up a sudden cheer—volley after volley.

From that night on Sim Dalt became famous as 'The goalie Bob Thropper could never beat!' The Arcade flourished. Sim got offers from many teams, including one from Hummerton club itself.

'When I join your club,' he told them, 'it'll not be as a goalie.'

And it was not many years before Sim's words came true, for there came a chance for him to buy a considerable portion of club shares, and he was voted a director.

One September morning early in the season he was taken round and introduced to all the players.

'Meet Bob Thropper,' said the co-director, 'our most famous centre-forward.'

Sim looked at the man before him. 'Centre-forwards,' he remarked significantly. 'I can buy 'em an' sell 'em—or,' he added, 'I can at least sell 'em.'

Some vague and long-forgotten moment of memory was evoked in Bob Thropper at these words.

He stood there frowning. Then, as Stan Mead nudged him and spoke, it all came back to him clearly.

'Bob, you'd better be looking for a nice pub to retire to,' Stan whispered feelingly, 'because this chap means it.'

Spit Nolan *by Bill Naughton*

Spit Nolan was a pal of mine. He was a thin lad with a bony
face that was always pale, except for two rosy spots on his
cheekbones. He had quick brown eyes, short wiry hair, rather
stooped shoulders, and we all knew that he had only one
lung. He had had a disease which in those days couldn't be
cured, unless you went away to Switzerland, which Spit
certainly couldn't afford. He wasn't sorry for himself in any
way, and in fact we envied him, because he never had to go
to school.

Spit was the champion trolley-rider of Cotton Pocket: that
was the district in which we lived. He had a very good
balance, and sharp wits, and he was very brave, so that these
qualities, when added to his skill as a rider, meant that no
other boy could ever beat Spit on a trolley—and every lad
had one.

Our trolleys were simple vehicles for getting a good ride
downhill at a fast speed. To make one you had to get a stout
piece of wood about five feet in length and eighteen inches
wide. Then you needed four wheels, preferably two pairs,
large ones for the back and smaller ones for the front.
However, since we bought our wheels from the scrapyard,
most trolleys had four odd wheels. Now you had to get a
poker and put it in the fire until it was red hot, and then
burn a hole through the wood at the front. Usually it would
take three or four attempts to get the hole bored through.
Through this hole you fitted the giant nut-and-bolt which
acted as a swivel for the steering. Fastened to the nut was a
strip of wood, onto which the front axle was secured by bent
nails. A piece of rope tied to each end of the axle served for
steering. Then a knob of margarine had to be slanced out of
the kitchen to grease the wheels and bearings. Next you had
to paint a name on it: *Invincible* or *Dreadnought*, though it

might be a motto: *Death before Dishonour* or *Labour and Wait.* That done, you then stuck your chest out, opened the back gate, and wheeled your trolley out to face the critical eyes of the world.

Spit spent most mornings trying out new speed gadgets on his trolley, or searching Enty's scrapyard for good wheels. Afternoons he would go off and have a spin down Cemetery Brew. This was a very steep road that led to the cemetery, and it was very popular with trolley-drivers as it was the only macadamized hill for miles around, all the others being cobblestones for horse traffic. Spit used to lie in wait for a coal-cart or other horse-drawn vehicle, then he would hitch *Egdam* to the back to take it up the brew. *Egdam* was a name in memory of a girl called Madge whom he had once met at Southport Sanatorium, when he had spent three happy weeks. Only I knew the meaning of it, for he had reversed the letters of her name to keep his love a secret.

It was the custom for lads to gather at the street corner on summer evenings and, trolleys parked at hand, discuss trolley-ing, road surfaces, and also show off any new gadgets. Then, when Spit gave the sign, we used to set off for Cemetery Brew. There was scarcely any evening traffic on the roads in those days, so that we could have a good practice before our evening race. Spit, the unbeaten champion, would inspect every trolley and rider, and allow a start which was reckoned on the size of the wheels and the weight of the rider. He was always the last in the line of starters, though no matter how long a start he gave, it seemed impossible to beat him. He knew that road like the palm of his hand, every tiny lump or pothole, and he never came a cropper.

Among us he took things easy, but when occasion asked for it he would go all out. Once he had to meet a challenge from Ducker Smith, the champion of the Engine Row gang. On that occasion Spit borrowed a wheel from the baby's pram, removing one nearest the wall so it wouldn't be missed, and confident he could replace it before his mother took baby out. And after fixing it to his trolley he made that ride on what was called the 'belly-down' style—that is, he lay full stretch on his stomach, so as to avoid wind resistance. Although Ducker got away to a flying start he had not that sensitive touch of Spit, and his frequent bumps and swerves lost him valuable inches, so that he lost the race by a good three lengths. Spit arrived home just in time to catch his mother as she was wheeling young Georgie off the doorstep, and if he had not made a dash for it the child would have fallen out as the pram overturned.

It happened that we were gathered at the street corner with our trolleys one evening when Ernie Haddock let out a hiccup of wonder: 'Hi, chaps, wot's Leslie got?'

We all turned our eyes on Leslie Duckett, the plump son of the local publican. He approached us on a brand-new trolley, propelled by flicks of his foot on the pavement. From a distance the thing had looked impressive, but now, when it came up among us, we were too dumbfounded to speak. Such a magnificent trolley had never been seen! The riding board was of solid oak, almost two inches thick; four new wheels with pneumatic tyres; a brake, a bell, a lamp, and a spotless steering-cord. In front was a plate on which was the name in bold lettering: *The British Queen*.

'It's called after the pub,' remarked Leslie. He tried to edge it away from Spit's trolley, for it made *Egdam* appear horribly insignificant. Voices had been stilled for a minute, but now they broke out:

'Where'd it come from?'

'How much was it?'

'Who made it?'

Leslie tried to look modest. 'My dad had it specially made to measure,' he said, 'by the gaffer of the Holt Engineering Works.'

He was a nice lad, and now he wasn't sure whether to feel proud or ashamed. The fact was, nobody had ever had a trolley made by somebody else. Trolleys were swopped and so on, but no lad had ever owned one that had been made by other hands. We went quiet now, for Spit had calmly turned his attention to it, and was examining *The British Queen* with his expert eye. First he tilted it, so that one of the rear wheels was off the ground, and after giving it a flick of the finger he listened intently with his ear close to the hub.

'A beautiful ball-bearing race,' he remarked, 'it runs like silk.' Next he turned his attention to the body. 'Grand piece of timber, Leslie—though a trifle on the heavy side. It'll take plenty of pulling up a brew.'

'I can pull it,' said Leslie, stiffening.

'You might find it a shade front-heavy,' went on Spit, 'which means it'll be hard on the steering unless you keep it well oiled.'

'It's well made,' said Leslie. 'Eh, Spit?'

Spit nodded. 'Aye, all the bolts are counter sunk,' he said, 'everything chamfered and fluted off to perfection. But—'

'But what?' asked Leslie.

'Do you want me to tell you?' asked Spit.

'Yes, I do,' answered Leslie.

'Well, it's got none of *you* in it,' said Spit.

'How do you mean?' said Leslie.

'Well, you haven't so much as given it a single tap with a hammer,' said Spit. 'That trolley will be a stranger to you to your dying day.'

'How come,' said Leslie, 'since I *own* it?'

Spit shook his head. 'You don't own it,' he said, in a quiet, solemn tone. 'You own nothing in this world except those things you have taken a hand in the making of, or else you've earned the money to buy them.'

Leslie sat down on *The British Queen* to think this one out. We all sat round, scratching our heads.

'You've forgotten to mention one thing,' said Ernie Haddock to Spit, 'what about the *speed?*'

'Going down a steep hill,' said Spit, 'she should hold the road well—an' with wheels like that she should certainly be able to shift some.'

'Think she could beat *Egdam?*' ventured Ernie.

'That,' said Spit, 'remains to be seen.'

Ernie gave a shout: 'A challenge race! *The British Queen* versus *Egdam!*'

'Not tonight,' said Leslie. 'I haven't got the proper feel of her yet.'

'What about Sunday morning?' I said.

Spit nodded. 'As good a time as any.'

Leslie agreed. 'By then,' he said in a challenging tone, 'I'll be able to handle her.'

Chattering like monkeys, eating bread, carrots, fruit, and bits of toffee, the entire gang of us made our way along the silent Sunday morning streets for the big race at Cemetery Brew. We were split into two fairly equal sides.

Leslie, in his serge Sunday suit, walked ahead, with Ernie Haddock pulling *The British Queen*, and a bunch of supporters around. They were optimistic, for Leslie had easily outpaced every other trolley during the week, though as yet he had not run against Spit.

Spit was in the middle of the group behind, and I was pulling *Egdam* and keeping the pace easy, for I wanted Spit to keep fresh. He walked in and out among us with an air of imperturbability that, considering the occasion, seemed almost godlike. It inspired a fanatical confidence in us. It was such that Chick Dale, a curly-headed kid with soft skin like a girl's and a nervous lisp, climbed up onto the spiked railings of the cemetery, and, reaching out with his thin fingers, snatched a yellow rose. He ran in front of Spit and thrust it into a small hole in his jersey.

'I pwesent you with the wose of the winner!' he exclaimed.

'And I've a good mind to present you with a clout on the lug,' replied Spit, 'for pinching a flower from a cemetery. An' what's more, it's bad luck.' Seeing Chick's face, he relented. 'On second thoughts, Chick, I'll wear it. Ee, wot a 'eavenly smell!'

Happily we went along, and Spit turned to a couple of lads at the back. 'Hi, stop that whistling. Don't forget what day it is—folk want their sleep out.'

A faint sweated glow had come over Spit's face when we

reached the top of the hill, but he was as majestically calm as ever. Taking the bottle of cold water from his trolley seat, he put it to his lips and rinsed out his mouth in the manner of a boxer.

The two contestants were called together by Ernie.

'No bumpin' or borin',' he said.

They nodded.

'The winner,' he said, 'is the first who puts the nose of his trolley past the cemetery gates.'

They nodded.

'Now, who,' he asked, 'is to be judge?'

Leslie looked at me. 'I've no objection to Bill,' he said. 'I know he's straight.'

I hadn't realised I was, I thought, but by heck I will be!

'Ernie here,' said Spit, 'can be starter.'

With that Leslie and Spit shook hands.

'Fly down to them gates,' said Ernie to me. He had his father's pigeon-timing watch in his hand. 'I'll be setting 'em off dead on the stroke of ten o'clock.'

I hurried down to the gates. I looked back and saw the supporters lining themselves on either side of the road. Leslie was sitting upright on *The British Queen*. Spit was settling himself to ride belly-down. Ernie Haddock, handkerchief raised in the right hand, eye gazing down on the watch in the left, was counting them off—just like when he tossed one of his father's pigeons.

'Five—four—three—two—one—OFF!'

Spit was away like a shot. That vigorous toe-push sent him clean ahead of Leslie. A volley of shouts went up from his supporters, and groans from Leslie's. I saw Spit move straight to the middle of the road camber. Then I ran ahead to take up my position at the winning-post.

When I turned again I was surprised to see that Spit had not increased the lead. In fact, it seemed that Leslie had begun to gain on him. He had settled himself into a crouched position, and those perfect wheels combined with his extra weight were bringing him up with Spit. Not that it seemed possible he could ever catch him. For Spit, lying flat on his trolley, moving with a fine balance, gliding, as it were, over the rough patches, looked to me as though he were a bird that might suddenly open out its wings and fly clean into the air.

The runners along the side could no longer keep up with the trolleys. And now, as they skimmed past the half-way mark, and came to the very steepest part, there was no doubt that Leslie was gaining. Spit had never ridden better: he coaxed *Egdam* over the tricky parts, swayed with her, gave her her head, and guided her. Yet Leslie, clinging grimly to the steering-rope of *The British Queen*, and riding the rougher part of the road, was actually drawing level. Those beautiful ball-bearing wheels, engineer-made, encased in oil, were holding the road, and bringing Leslie along faster than spirit and skill could carry Spit.

Dead level they sped into the final stretch. Spit's slight figure was poised fearlessly on his trolley, drawing the extremes of speed from her. Thundering beside him, anxious but determined, came Leslie. He was actually drawing ahead—and forcing his way to the top of the camber. On they came like two charioteers—Spit delicately edging to the side to gain inches by the extra downward momentum. I kept my eyes fastened clean across the road as they came belting past the winning-post.

First past was the plate *The British Queen*. I saw that first. Then I saw the heavy rear wheel jog over a pothole and strike Spit's front wheel—sending him in a swerve across the road. Suddenly then, from nowhere, a charabanc came speeding round the wide bend.

Spit was straight in its path. Nothing could avoid the collision. I gave a cry of fear as I saw the heavy solid tyre of the front wheel hit the trolley. Spit was flung up and his back hit the radiator. Then the driver stopped dead.

I got there first. Spit was lying on the macadam road on his side. His face was white and dusty, and coming out between his lips and trickling down his chin was a rivulet of fresh red blood. Scattered all about him were yellow rose petals.

'Not my fault,' I heard the driver shouting. 'I didn't have a chance. He came straight at me.'

The next thing we were surrounded by women who had got out of the charabanc. And then Leslie and all the lads came up.

'Somebody send for an ambulance!' called a woman.

'I'll run an' tell the gatekeeper to telephone,' said Ernie Haddock.

'I hadn't got a chance,' the driver explained to the women.

'A piece of his jersey on the starting-handle there . . .' said someone.

'Don't move him,' said the driver to a stout woman who had bent over Spit. 'Wait for the ambulance.'

'Hush up,' she said. She knelt and put a silk scarf under Spit's head. Then she wiped his mouth with her little handkerchief.

He opened his eyes. Glazed they were, as though he couldn't see. A short cough came out of him, then he looked at me and his lips moved.

'Who won?'

'Thee!' blurted out Leslie. 'Tha just licked me. Eh, Bill?'

'Aye,' I said, 'old *Egdam* just pipped *The British Queen*.'

Spit's eyes closed again. The women looked at each other. They nearly all had tears in their eyes. Then Spit looked up again, and his wise, knowing look came over his face. After a minute he spoke in a sharp whisper:

'Liars. I can remember seeing Leslie's back wheel hit my front 'un. I didn't win—I lost.' He stared upward for a few seconds, then his eyes twitched and shut.

The driver kept repeating how it wasn't his fault, and next thing the ambulance came. Nearly all the women were crying now, and I saw the look that went between the two men who put Spit on a stretcher—but I couldn't believe he was dead. I had to go into the ambulance with the attendant to give him particulars. I went up the step and sat down inside and looked out the little window as the driver slammed the doors. I saw the driver holding Leslie as a witness. Chick Dale was lifting

the smashed-up *Egdam* onto the body of *The British Queen.*
People with bunches of flowers in their hands stared after us
as we drove off. Then I heard the ambulance man asking me
Spit's name. Then he touched me on the elbow with his pencil
and said:

'Where did he live?'

I knew then. That word 'did' struck right into me. But for
a minute I couldn't answer. I had to think hard, for the way
he said it made it suddenly seem as though Spit Nolan had
been dead and gone for ages.

A Message from the Pig-man

by John Wain

He was never called Ekky now, because he was getting to be
a real boy, nearly six, with grey flannel trousers that had a
separate belt, and weren't kept up by elastic, and his name
was Eric. But this was just one of those changes brought about
naturally, by time, not a disturbing alteration; he understood
that. His mother hadn't meant that kind of change when she
had promised, 'Nothing will be changed.' It was all going to
go on as before, except that Dad wouldn't be there, and
Donald would be there instead. He knew Donald, of course,
and felt all right about his being in the house, though it
seemed, when he lay in bed and thought about it, mad and
pointless that Donald's coming should mean that Dad had to
go. Why should it mean that? The house was quite big. He
hadn't any brothers and sisters, and if he *had* had any he
wouldn't have minded sharing his bedroom, even with a baby
that wanted a lot of looking after, so long as it left the spare
room free for Dad to sleep in. If he did that, they wouldn't
have a spare room, it was true, but then, the spare room was
nearly always empty; the last time anybody had used the spare
room was *years* ago, when he had been much smaller—last
winter, in fact. And, even then, the visitor, the lady with the
funny teeth who laughed as she breathed in, instead of as she
breathed out like everyone else, had only stayed two or three
nights. *Why* did grown-ups do everything in such a mad, silly
way? They often told him not to be silly, but they were silly
themselves in a useless way, not laughing or singing or
anything, just being silly and sad.

It was hard to read the signs; that was another thing. When
they did give you something to go on, it was impossible to
know how to take it. Dad had bought him a train, just a few
weeks ago, and taught him how to fit the lines together. That
ought to have meant that he would stay; what sensible person

would buy a train, and fit it all up ready to run, even as a present for another person—*and then leave?* Donald had been quite good about the train, Eric had to admit that; he had bought a bridge for it and a lot of rolling-stock. At first he had got the wrong kind of rolling-stock, with wheels too close together to fit onto the rails; but instead of playing the usual grown-ups' trick of pulling a face and then not doing anything about it, he had gone back to the shop, straight away that same afternoon, and got the right kind. Perhaps that meant *he* was going to leave. But that didn't seem likely. Not the way Mum held onto him all the time, even holding him round the middle as if he needed keeping in one piece.

All the same, he was not Ekky now, he was Eric, and he was sensible and grown-up. Probably it was his own fault that everything seemed strange. He was not living up to his grey flannel trousers—perhaps that was it; being afraid of too many things, not asking questions that would probably turn out to have quite simple answers.

The Pig-man, for instance. He had let the Pig-man worry him far too much. None of the grown-ups acted as if the Pig-man was anything to be afraid of. He probably just *looked* funny, that was all. If, instead of avoiding him so carefully, he went outside one evening and looked at him, took a good long, unafraid look, leaving the back door open behind him so that he could dart in to the safety and warmth of the house . . . no! It was better, after all, not to see the Pig-man; not till he was bigger, anyway; nearly six was quite big but it wasn't really *very* big . . .

And yet it was one of those puzzling things. No-one ever told him to be careful not to let the Pig-man get hold of him, or warned him in any way; so the Pig-man *must* be harmless, because when it came to anything that *could* hurt you, like the traffic on the main road, people were always ramming it into you that you must look both ways, and all that stuff. And yet when it came to the Pig-man, no-one ever mentioned him; he seemed beneath the notice of grown-ups. His mother would say now and then, 'Let me see, it's today the Pig-man comes, isn't it?' or, 'Oh dear, the Pig-man will be coming round soon, and I haven't put anything out.' If she talked like this, Eric's spine would tingle and go cold; he would keep very still and wait, because quite often her next words would be, 'Eric, just take these peelings,' or whatever it was, 'out to the bucket, dear, will you?' The bucket was about fifty yards away from the back door: it was shared by the people in the two next-door houses. None of *them* was afraid of the Pig-man either. What was their attitude, he wondered? Were they sorry for him, having to eat damp old stuff out of a bucket—tea-leaves and eggshells and that sort of thing? Perhaps he cooked it when he got home, and made it a bit nicer. Certainly, it didn't look too nice when you lifted the lid of the bucket and saw it all lying there. It sometimes smelt, too. Was the Pig-man very poor? Was he sorry for himself, or did he feel all right about being like that? *Like what?* What did the Pig-man look like? He would have little eyes and a snout with a flat end; but would he have trotters, or hands and feet like a person's?

Lying on his back, Eric worked soberly at the problem. The Pig-man's bucket had a handle; so he must carry it in the ordinary way, in his hand—unless, of course, he walked on all fours and carried it in his mouth. But that wasn't very likely, because if he walked on all fours, what difference would there be between him and an ordinary pig? To be called the Pig-man, rather than the Man-pig, surely implied that he was upright, and dressed. Could he talk? Probably, in a kind of grunting way, or else how would he tell the people what kind of food he wanted them to put in his bucket? *Why hadn't he asked Dad about the Pig-man?* That had been his mistake; Dad would have told him exactly all about it. But he had gone. Eric fell asleep, and in his sleep he saw Dad and the Pig-man going in a train together: he called, but they did not hear him and the train carried them away. 'Dad!' he shouted desperately after it. 'Don't bring the Pig-man when you come back! Don't bring the Pig-man!' Then his mother was in the room, kissing him and smelling nice; she felt soft, and the softness ducked him into sleep, this time without dreams, but the next day his questions returned.

Still, there was school in the morning, and going down to the swings in the afternoon, and altogether a lot of different things to crowd out the figure of the Pig-man and the questions connected with it. And he was never further from worrying about it all than that moment, a few evenings later, when it suddenly came to a crisis.

Eric had been allowed 'just for once' to bring his train into the dining-room after tea, because there was a fire there that made it nicer than the room where he usually played. It was warm and bright, and the carpet in front of the fireplace was smooth and firm, exactly right for laying out the rails on. Donald had come home and was sitting—in Dad's chair, but never mind—reading the paper and smoking. Mum was in the kitchen, clattering gently about, and both doors were open so that she and Donald could call out remarks to each other. Only a short passage lay between. It was just the part of the day Eric liked best, and bedtime was comfortably far off. He fitted the sections of rail together, glancing in anticipation at the engine as it stood proudly waiting to haul the carriages round and round, tremendously fast.

Then his mother called, 'Eric! Do be a sweet, good boy, and take this stuff out to the Pig-man. My hands are covered with cake mixture. I'll let you scrape out the basin when you come in.'

For a moment he kept quite still, hoping he hadn't really heard her say it, that it was just a voice inside his head. But Donald looked over at him and said, 'Go along, old man. You don't mind, do you?'

Eric said, 'But tonight's when the Pig-man comes.'

Surely, *surely* they weren't asking him to go out in the deep twilight, just at the time when there was the greatest danger of actually *meeting* the Pig-man.

'All the better,' said Donald, turning back to his paper.

Why was it better? Did they *want* him to meet the Pig-man? Slowly, wondering why his feet and legs didn't refuse to move,

Eric went through into the kitchen. 'There it is,' his mother said, pointing to a brown-paper carrier full of potato-peelings and scraps.

He took it up and opened the back door. If he was quick and darted along to the bucket *at once*, he would be able to lift the lid, throw the stuff in quickly, and be back in the house in about the time it took to count ten.

One—two—three—four—five—six. He stopped. The bucket wasn't there.

It had gone. Eric peered round, but the light, though faint, was not as faint as *that*. He could see that the bucket had gone. *The Pig-man had already been.*

Seven—eight—nine—ten, his steps were joyous and light. Back in the house, where it was warm and bright and his train was waiting.

'The Pig-man's gone, Mum. The bucket's not there.'

She frowned, hands deep in the pudding-basin. 'Oh, yes, I do believe I heard him. But it was only a moment ago. Yes, it was just before I called you, darling. It must have been that that made me think of it.'

'Yes?' he said politely, putting down the carrier.

'So if you nip along, dear, you can easily catch him up. And I *do* want that stuff out of the way.'

'Catch him up?' he asked, standing still in the doorway.

'Yes, dear, *catch him up*,' she answered rather sharply (the Efficient Young Mother knows when to be Firm). 'He can't possibly be more than a very short way down the road.'

Before she had finished Eric was outside the door and running. This was a technique he knew. It was the same as getting into icy cold water. If it was the end, if the Pig-man seized him by the hand and dragged him off to his hut, well, so much the worse. Swinging the paper carrier in his hand, he ran fast through the dusk.

The back view of the Pig-man was much as he had expected it to be. A slow, rather lurching gait, hunched shoulders, an old hat crushed down on his head (to hide his ears?) and the pail in his hand. Plod, plod, as if he were tired. Perhaps this was just a ruse, though probably he could pounce quickly enough when his wicked little eyes saw a nice tasty little boy or something . . . did the Pig-man eat birds? Or cats?

Eric stopped. He opened his mouth to call to the Pig-man, but the first time he tried, nothing came out except a small rasping squeak. His heart was banging like fireworks going off. He could hardly hear anything.

'Mr Pig-man!' he called, and this time the words came out clear and rather high.

The jogging old figure stopped, turned, and looked at him. Eric could not see properly from where he stood. But he *had* to see. Everything, even his fear, sank and drowned in the raging tide of his curiosity. He moved forward. With each step he saw more clearly. The Pig-man was just an ordinary old man.

'Hello, sonny. Got some stuff there for the old grunters?'

Eric nodded, mutely, and held out his offering. What old grunters? What did he mean?

The Pig-man put down his bucket. He had ordinary hands, ordinary arms. He took the lid off. Eric held out the paper carrier, and the Pig-man's hand actually touched his own for a second. A flood of gratitude rose up inside him. The Pig-man tipped the scraps into the bucket and handed the carrier back.

'Thanks, sonny,' he said.

'Who's it for?' Eric asked, with another rush of articulateness. His voice seemed to have a life of its own.

The Pig-man straightened up, puzzled. Then he laughed, in a gurgling sort of way, but not like a pig at all.

'Arh Aarh Harh Harh,' the Pig-man went. 'Not for me, if that's whatcher mean, arh, harh.'

He put the lid back on the bucket. 'It's for the old grunters,' he said. 'The old porkers. Just what they likes. Only not fruit-skins. I leaves a note, sometimes, about what not to put in. Never fruit-skins. It gives 'em the belly-ache.'

He was called the Pig-man because he had some pigs that he looked after.

'Thank you,' said Eric. 'Goodnight.' He ran back towards

the house, hearing the Pig-man, the ordinary old man, the ordinary usual normal old man, say in his just ordinary old man's voice, 'Goodnight, sonny.'

So that was how you did it. You just went straight ahead, not worrying about this or that. Like getting into cold water. You just *did* it.

He slowed down as he got to the gate. For instance, if there was a question that you wanted to know the answer to, and you had always just felt you couldn't ask, the thing to do was to ask it. Just straight out, like going up to the Pig-man. Difficult things, troubles, questions, you just treated them like the Pig-man.

So that was it!

The warm light shone through the crack of the door. He opened it and went in. His mother was standing at the table, her hands still working the cake mixture about. She would let him scrape out the basin, and the spoon—he would ask for the spoon, too. But not straight away. There was a more important thing first.

He put the paper carrier down and went up to her. 'Mum,' he said. 'Why can't Dad be with us even if Donald *is* here? I mean, why can't he live with us as well as Donald?'

His mother turned and went to the sink. She put the tap on and held her hands under it.

'Darling,' she called.

'Yes?' came Donald's voice.

'D'you know what he's just said?'

'What?'

'He's just asked . . .' She turned the tap off and dried her hands, not looking at Eric. 'He wants to know why we can't have Jack to live with us.'

There was a silence, then Donald said quietly, so that his voice only just reached Eric's ears, 'That's a hard one.'

'You can scrape out the basin,' his mother said to Eric. She lifted him up and kissed him. Then she rubbed her cheek along his, leaving a wet smear. 'Poor little Ekky,' she said in a funny voice.

She put him down and he began to scrape out the pudding-basin, certain at least of one thing, that grown-ups were mad and silly and he hated them all, all, *all*.

The Fun They Had *by Isaac Asimov*

Margie even wrote about it that night in her diary. On the page headed May 17, 2155, she wrote, 'Today Tommy found a real book!'

It was a very old book. Margie's grandfather once said that when he was a little boy *his* grandfather told him that there was a time when all stories were printed on paper.

They turned the pages, which were yellow and crinkly, and it was awfully funny to read words that stood still instead of moving the way they were supposed to—on a screen, you know. And then, when they turned back to the page before, it had the same words on it that it had had when they read it the first time.

'Gee,' said Tommy, 'what a waste. When you're through the book, you just throw it away, I guess. Our television screen must have had a million books on it and it's good for plenty more. I wouldn't throw *it* away.'

'Same with mine,' said Margie. She was eleven and hadn't seen as many telebooks as Tommy had. He was thirteen.

She said, 'Where did you find it?'

'In my house.' He pointed without looking, because he was busy reading. 'In the attic.'

'What's it about?'

'School.'

Margie was scornful. 'School? What's there to write about school? I hate school.' Margie always hated school, but now she hated it more than ever. The mechanical teacher had been giving her test after test in geography and she had been doing worse and worse until her mother had shaken her head sorrowfully and sent for the County Inspector.

He was a round little man with a red face and a whole box of tools with dials and wires. He smiled at her and gave her an apple, then took the teacher apart. Margie had hoped he wouldn't know how to put it together again, but he knew how all right and after an hour or so, there it was again, large and black and ugly with a big screen on which all the lessons were shown and the questions were asked. That wasn't so bad. The part she hated most was the slot where she had to put homework and test papers. She always had to write them out in a punch code they made her learn when she was six years old, and the mechanical teacher calculated the mark in no time.

The Inspector had smiled after he had finished and patted her head. He said to her mother, 'It's not the little girl's fault, Mrs Jones. I think the geography sector was geared a little too quick. These things happen sometimes. I've slowed it up to an average ten-year level. Actually, the overall pattern of her progress is quite satisfactory.' And he patted Margie's head again.

Margie was disappointed. She had been hoping they would take the teacher away altogether. They had once taken Tommy's teacher away for nearly a month because the history sector had blanked out completely.

So she said to Tommy, 'Why would anyone write about school?'

Tommy looked at her with very superior eyes. 'Because it's not our kind of school, stupid. This is the old kind of school that they had hundreds and hundreds of years ago.' He added loftily, pronouncing the word carefully, '*Centuries* ago.'

Margie was hurt. 'Well, I don't know what kind of school they had all that time ago.' She read the book over his shoulder for a while, then said, 'Anyway, they had a teacher.'

'Sure they had a teacher, but it wasn't a *regular* teacher. It was a man.'

'A man? How could a man be a teacher?'

'Well, he just told the boys and girls things and gave them homework and asked them questions.'

'A man isn't smart enough.'

'Sure he is. My father knows as much as my teacher.'

'He can't. A man can't know as much as a teacher.'

'He knows almost as much, I betcha.'

Margie wasn't prepared to dispute that. She said, 'I wouldn't want a strange man in my house to teach me.'

Tommy screamed with laughter. 'You don't know much, Margie. The teachers didn't live in the house. They had a special building and all the kids went there.'

'And all the kids learned the same thing?'

'Sure, if they were the same age.'

'But my mother says a teacher has to be adjusted to fit the mind of each boy and girl it teaches and that each kid has to be taught differently.'

'Just the same they didn't do it that way then. If you don't like it, you don't have to read the book.'

'I didn't say I didn't like it,' Margie said quickly. She wanted to read about those funny schools.

They weren't even half finished when Margie's mother called 'Margie! School!'

Margie looked up. 'Not yet, mamma.'

'Now,' said Mrs Jones. 'And it's probably time for Tommy, too.'

Margie said to Tommy, 'Can I read the book some more with you after school?'

'Maybe,' he said, nonchalantly. He walked away whistling, the dusty old book tucked beneath his arm.

Margie went into the school-room. It was right next to her bedroom, and the mechanical teacher was on and waiting for her. It was always on at the same time every day except Saturday and Sunday, because her mother said little girls learned better if they learned at regular hours.

The screen was lit up, and it said: 'Today's arithmetic lesson is on the addition of proper fractions. Please insert yesterday's homework in the proper slot.'

Margie did so with a sigh. She was thinking about the old schools they had when her grandfather's grandfather was a little boy. All the kids from the whole neighbourhood came, laughing and shouting in the schoolyard, sitting together in the school-room, going home together at the end of the day.

They learned the same things so they could help one another on the homework and talk about it.

And the teachers were people.

The mechanical teacher was flashing on the screen: 'When we add the fractions ½ and ¼ —'

Margie was thinking about how the kids must have loved it in the old days. She was thinking about the fun they had.

The Night the Ghost Got In

by *James Thurber*

The ghost that got into our house on the night of 17 November 1915 raised such a hullabaloo of misunderstandings that I am sorry I didn't just let it keep on walking, and go to bed. Its advent caused my mother to throw a shoe through a window of the house next door and ended up with my grandfather shooting a patrolman. I am sorry, therefore, as I have said, that I ever paid any attention to the footsteps.

They began about a quarter past one o'clock in the morning, a rhythmic, quick-cadenced walking around the dining-room table. My mother was asleep in one room upstairs, my brother Herman in another; grandfather was in the attic, in the old walnut bed which, as you will remember, once fell on my father. I had just stepped out of the bathtub and was busily rubbing myself with a towel when I heard the steps. They were the steps of a man walking rapidly around the dining-room table downstairs. The light from the bathroom shone down the back steps, which dropped directly into the dining-room; I could see the faint shine of plates on the plate-rail; I couldn't see the table. The steps kept going round and round the table; at regular intervals a board creaked, when it was trod upon. I supposed at first that it was my father or my brother Roy, who had gone to Indianapolis but were expected home at any time. I suspected next that it was a burglar. It did not enter my mind until later that it was a ghost.

After the walking had gone on for perhaps three minutes, I tiptoed to Herman's room. 'Psst!' I hissed, in the dark, shaking him. 'Awp,' he said, in the low, hopeless tone of a despondent beagle—he always half suspected that something would 'get him' in the night. I told him who I was. 'There's something downstairs!' I said. He got up and followed me to the head of the back staircase. We listened together. There was no sound. The steps had ceased. Herman looked at me in some alarm: I had only the bath towel around my waist. He wanted to go back to bed, but I gripped his arm. 'There's something down there!' I said. Instantly the steps began again, circled the dining-room table like a man running, and started up the stairs towards us, heavily, two at a time. The light still shone palely down the stairs; we saw nothing coming; we only heard the steps. Herman rushed to his room and slammed the door. I slammed shut the door at the stairs top and held my knee against it. After a long minute, I slowly opened it again. There was nothing there. There was no sound. None of us ever heard the ghost again.

The slamming of the doors had aroused mother: she peered out of her room. 'What on earth are you boys doing?' she demanded. Herman ventured out of his room. 'Nothing,' he said gruffly, but he was, in colour, a light green. 'What was all that running around downstairs?' said mother. So she had heard the steps, too! We just looked at her. 'Burglars!' she shouted intuitively. I tried to quiet her by starting lightly downstairs.

'Come on, Herman,' I said.

'I'll stay with mother,' he said. 'She's all excited.'

I stepped back onto the landing.

'Don't either of you go a step,' said mother. 'We'll call the police.' Since the phone was downstairs, I didn't see how we were going to call the police—nor did I want the police—but mother made one of her quick, incomparable decisions. She flung up a window of her bedroom, which faced the bedroom windows of the house of a neighbour, picked up a shoe, and whammed it through a pane of glass across the narrow space that separated the two houses. Glass tinkled into the bedroom occupied by a retired engraver named Bodwell and his wife. Bodwell had been for some years in rather a bad way and was subject to mild 'attacks'. Most everybody we knew or lived near had *some* kind of attacks.

It was now about two o'clock of a moonless night; clouds hung black and low. Bodwell was at the window in a minute, shouting, frothing a little, shaking his fist. 'We'll sell the house and go back to Peoria,' we could hear Mrs Bodwell saying. It was some time before mother 'got through' to Bodwell. 'Burglars!' she shouted. 'Burglars in the house!' Herman and I hadn't dared to tell her that it was not burglars but ghosts, for she was even more afraid of ghosts than of burglars. Bodwell at first thought that she meant there were burglars in his house, but finally he quieted down and called the police for us over an extension phone by his bed. After he had disappeared from the window, mother suddenly made as if to throw another shoe, not because there was further need of it but, as she later explained, because the thrill of heaving a shoe through a window glass had enormously taken her fancy. I prevented her.

The police were on hand in a commendably short time: a Ford sedan full of them, two on motor-cycles, and a patrol wagon with about eight in it and a few reporters. They began banging at our front door. Flashlights shot streaks of gleam up and down the walls, across the yard, down the walk between our house and Bodwell's. 'Open up!' cried a hoarse voice. 'We're men from Headquarters!' I wanted to go down and let them in, since there they were, but mother wouldn't hear of it. 'You haven't a stitch on,' she pointed out. 'You'd catch your death.' I wound the towel around me again. Finally the cops put their shoulders to our big heavy front door with its thick bevelled glass and broke it in: I could hear a rending of wood and splash of glass on the floor of the hall. Their lights played all over the living-room and criss-crossed nervously in the dining-room, stabbed into the hallways, shot up the front stairs and finally up the back. They caught me standing in my towel at the top. A heavy policeman bounded up the steps. 'Who are you?' he demanded. 'I live here,' I said. 'Well, whattsa matta, ya hot?' he asked. It was, as a matter of fact, cold; I went to my room and pulled on some trousers. On my way out, a cop stuck a gun into my ribs. 'Whatta you doin' here' he demanded. 'I live here,' I said.

The officer in charge reported to mother. 'No sign of nobody, lady,' he said. 'Musta got away—whatt'd he look like?' There were two or three of them,' mother said, 'whooping and carrying on and slamming doors.' 'Funny,' said the cop. 'All ya windows and doors was locked on the inside tight as a tick.' Downstairs, we could hear the tromping of the other police. Police were all over the place; doors were yanked open, drawers were yanked open, windows were shot up and pulled down, furniture fell with dull thumps. A half-dozen policemen emerged out of the darkness of the front hallway upstairs. They began to ransack the floor: pulled beds away from walls, tore clothes off hooks in the closets, pulled suitcases and boxes off shelves. One of them found an old zither that Roy had won in a pool tournament. 'Looky here, Joe,' he said strumming it with a big paw. The cop named Joe took it and turned it over. 'What is it?' he asked me. 'It's an old zither our guinea-pig used to sleep on,' I said. It was true that a pet guinea-pig we once had would never sleep anywhere except on the zither, but I should never have said so. Joe and the other cop looked at me a long time. They put the zither back on a shelf.

'No sign o'nuthin',' said the cop who had first spoken to mother. 'This guy,' he explained to the others, jerking a thumb at me, 'was nekked. The lady seems historical.' They all nodded, but said nothing; just looked at me. In the small silence we all heard a creaking in the attic. Grandfather was turning over in bed. 'What's 'at?' snapped Joe. Five or six cops sprang for the attic door before I could intervene or explain. I realised that it would be bad if they burst in on grandfather unannounced or even announced. He was going through a phase in which he believed that General Meade's men, under steady hammering by Stonewall Jackson, were beginning to retreat and even desert.

When I got to the attic, things were pretty confused. Grandfather had evidently jumped to the conclusion that the police were deserters from Meade's army, trying to hide away in his attic. He bounded out of bed wearing a long flannel nightgown over long woollen underwear, a nightcap, and a leather jacket around his chest. The cops must have realised at once that the indignant white-haired old man belonged in the house, but they had no chance to say so. 'Back, ye cowardl‹ dogs!' roared grandfather. 'Back t' the lines, ye goddam lily livered cattle!' With that, he fetched the officer who found th‹ zither a flat-handed smack alongside his head that sent hin sprawling. The others beat a retreat, but not fast enough grandfather grabbed Zither's gun from its holster and let fly The report seemed to crack the rafters; smoked filled the attic A cop cursed and shot his hand to his shoulder. Somehow, w‹ all finally got downstairs again and locked the door agains the old gentleman. He fired once or twice more in the darknes: and then went back to bed. 'That was grandfather,' I explainec to Joe, out of breath. 'He thinks you're deserters.' 'I'll say h‹ does,' said Joe.

The cops were reluctant to leave without getting their hand‹ on somebody besides grandfather; the night had been distinctl‹ a defeat for them. Furthermore, they obviously didn't like th‹ 'layout', something looked—and I can see thei‹ viewpoint—phoney. They began to poke into things again. A reporter, a thin-faced, wispy man, came up to me. I had pu‹ on one of mother's blouses, not being able to find anything else. The reporter looked at me with mingled suspicion and interest. 'Just what the hell is the real lowdown here, Bud?' he asked. I decided to be frank with him. 'We had ghosts,' I said. He gazed at me a long time as if I were a slot-machine into which he had, without results, dropped a nickel. Then he walked away. The cops followed him, the one grandfather sho‹ holding his now-bandaged arm, cursing and blaspheming. 'I'm gonna get my gun back from that old bird,' said the zither-cop. 'Yeh,' said Joe. 'You—and who else?' I told them I would bring it to the station house the next day.

'What was the matter with that one policeman?' mother asked, after they had gone. 'Grandfather shot him,' I said. 'What for?' she demanded. I told her he was a deserter. 'Of all things!' said mother. 'He was such a nice-looking young man.'

Grandfather was fresh as a daisy and full of jokes at breakfast next morning. We thought at first he had forgotten all about what had happened, but he hadn't. Over his third cup of coffee, he glared at Herman and me. 'What was the idee of all them cops tarryhootin' round the house last night?' he demanded. He had us there.

Mr Monroe Outwits a Bat

by James Thurber

The Monroes opened their summer place a little late, for carking cares had kept them long in town. The grass was greening and tangled when they arrived, and the house had a woodsy smell. Mr Monroe took a deep breath. 'I'll get a great sleep tonight,' he said. He put on some old clothes, pottered around inspecting doors and windows, whistling. After dinner he went out under the stars and smelled the clear fine air. Abruptly there came to his ears a little scream from inside the house—the scream his wife gave when she dropped a cup or when some other trivial tragedy of the kitchen occurred. Mr Monroe hurried inside.

'Spider!' cried Mrs Monroe. 'Oh, kill it, kill it!' She always held that a spider, encountered but not slain turned up in one's bed at night. Mr Monroe loved to kill spiders for his wife. He whacked this one off a tea-towel with a newspaper, and scooped it outside the door into the petunia bed. It gave him a feeling of power, and enhanced the sweetness of his little wife's dependence on him. He was still glowing with his triumph, in a small, warm way, when he went to bed.

'Goodnight dear,' he called, deeply. His voice was always a little deeper than usual, after a triumph.

'Goodnight dear,' she called back from her room.

The night was sweet and clear. Nice old creaking sounds ran down the steps and back up again. Some of them sounded like the steps of a person.

'Afraid, dear?' he called out.

'Not with you here,' she answered sleepily. There was a long pleasant silence. Mr Monroe began to drowse. A very ominous sound brought him out of it, a distinct flut, a firm, insistent, rhythmic flut.

'Bat!' muttered Mr Monroe to himself.

At first he took the advent of the bat calmly. It seemed to be flying high, near the ceiling. He even boldly raised up on his elbows and peered through the dark. As he did so the bat, apparently out of sheer malice, almost clipped the top of his head. Mr Monroe scrambled under the covers, but instantly recovered his composure and put his head out again—just as the bat, returning on its orbit, skimmed across the bed once more. Mr Monroe pulled the covers over his head. It was the bat's round.

'Restless, dear?' called his wife, through her open door.

'What?' he said.

'Why, what's the matter?' she asked, slightly alarmed at his muffled tone.

'I'm all right, it's okay,' responded Mr Monroe, from under the covers.

'You sound funny,' said his wife. There was a pause.

'Goodnight dear?' called Mr Monroe, poking his head out to say this, and pulling it in again.

'Goodnight.'

He strained his ears to hear through the covers, and found he could. The bat was still flitting above the bed in measured, relentless intervals. The notion came to the warm and stuffy Mr Monroe that the incessant repetition of a noise at regular intervals might drive a person crazy. He dismissed the thought, or tried to. If the dripping of water on a man's head, slowly, drip, drip, drip—flut, flut, flut—

'Damn it,' said Mr Monroe to himself. The bat was apparently just getting into its swing. It was flying faster. The first had just been practice. Mr Monroe suddenly bethought himself of a great spread of mosquito netting lying in a closet across the room. If he could get that and put it over the bed, he could sleep in peace. He poked his nose out from under the sheet, reached out a hand, and stealthily felt around for a match on a table by the bed—the lightswitch was yards away. Gradually his head and shoulders emerged. The bat seemed to be waiting for just this move. It zipped past his cheek. He flung himself back under the covers, with a great squeaking of springs.

'John?' called his wife.

'What's the matter now?' he asked querulously.

'What *are* you doing?' she demanded.

'There's a bat in the room, if you want to know,' he said, 'and it keeps scraping the covers.'

'Scraping the covers?'

'Yes, scraping the covers.'

'It'll go away,' said his wife. 'They go away.'

'I'll drive it away!' shouted John Monroe, for his wife's tone was that of a mother addressing a child.

'How the devil the damn bat ever . . .' his voice grew dim because he was now pretty far under the bed clothes.

'I can't hear you, dear,' said Mrs Monroe. He popped his head out.

'I say how long is it before they go away?' he asked.

'It'll hang by its feet pretty soon and go to sleep,' said his wife, soothingly. 'It won't hurt you.' This last had a curious effect on Mr Monroe. Much to his own surprise he sat upright in bed, a little angry. The bat actually got him this time, brushed his hair with a little 'Squeep!'

'Hey!' yelled Mr Monroe.

'What is it dear?' called his wife. He leaped out of bed, now completely panic-stricken, and ran for his wife's room. He went in and closed the door behind him, and stood there.

'Get in with me, dear,' said Mrs Monroe.

'I'm all right,' he retorted, irritably. 'I simply want to get something to rout that thing with. I couldn't find anything in my room.' He flicked on the lights.

'There's no sense in your getting all worn out fighting a bat,' said his wife. 'They're terribly quick.' There seemed to him to be an amused sparkle in her eyes.

'Well, I'm terribly quick too,' grumbled Mr Monroe, trying to keep from shivering, and he slowly folded a newspaper into a sort of club. With this in his hand he stepped to the door. 'I'll shut your door after me,' he said, 'so the bat won't get in your room.' He went out, firmly closing the door behind him. He crept slowly along the hall till he came to his own room.

He waited a while and listened. The bat was still going strong. Mr Monroe lifted the paper club and struck the jamb of the door, from the outside, a terrific blow. 'Wham!' went the blow. He hit again, 'Wham!'

'Did you get it, dear?' called his wife, her voice coming dimly through the door.

'Okay,' cried her husband, 'I got it.' He waited a long while. Then he slipped, on tiptoe, to a couch in the corridor halfway between his room and his wife's and gently, ever so gently, let himself down upon it. He slept lightly, because he was pretty chilly, until dawn, then got up and tiptoed to his room. He peered in. The bat was gone. Mr Monroe got into bed and went to sleep.

Notes

THE BOY AND THE BADGER

8 *champed*: bitten, gnawed at
11 *tow-topped*: covered with coarse, tousled hair

GRUMPHIE

15 *progeny*: children
red-polled: red-headed
18 *pennant*: long tapering flag

RATS

26 *ferret*: half-tamed type of polecat used for hunting rats or rabbits
27 *sovereigns*: gold coins originally worth £1
28 *vats, hogsheads, demijohns*: tubs, casks, bottles
32 *Poplar*: a (former) borough of London

LOST AND FOUND

34 *veldschoens*: shoes made of soft hide
dorp: village or town
brey: soften
35 *magtig!*: good gracious!
kraal: cattle-enclosure
mealies: corn
spruit: stream
36 *veld*: grassland
38 *konfyt*: jam
39 *blue-gum*: tree
40 *meneer*: sir
jong: young man
43 *voorslag*: that part of the whip that lashes
46 *ons*: our

Notes

THE PARSLEY GARDEN
49 *faucet*: tap
okra: plant whose seed-pods are used in soups
52 *Fresno*: in California

JENNY
69 *Baldor*: (Baldur or Balder) Scandinavian god of light
Thor: Scandinavian god of thunder (Thor's day = Thursday)
Wodin: (Woden, Wodan or Odin) Scandinavian god of war (Woden's day = Wednesday)
Leif Ericson: 11th century Norwegian explorer, believed to be the first European to reach North America

SPIT NOLAN
94 *macadamized*: (road) surfaced with asphalt or tar
brew: steep hill
95 *pneumatic*: inflated with air
96 *chamfered and fluted*: cut smooth and grooved
97 *serge*: hard-wearing material used for suits
98 *camber*: convex curve or slope of the road
99 *charabanc*: motor coach or bus

THE NIGHT THE GHOST GOT IN
117 *zither*: a flat many-stringed musical instrument
historical: malapropism for 'hysterical'
General Meade; Stonewall Jackson: generals on opposing sides in the American Civil War (1861–1865)
118 *nickel*: a 5 cent piece

MR MONROE OUTWITS A BAT
120 *carking*: worrying, vexatious
123 *jamb*: the upright or sidepost of the door frame

Teacher's Note

Reading Aloud

The stories are usually best enjoyed when read aloud. The reading should be strong and uninterrupted, bringing out where necessary the dialectal flavour. Difficult vocabulary should be simplified (*eg* by substituting 'steep hill' for 'brew' in *Spit Nolan*) and technical terms should be explained without breaking the flow of the story. Obscure references are explained in the Notes and can be jotted down in the teacher's copy before the lesson.

Discussion

This need not follow immediately, but after a short cathartic pause. If the story has had a strong emotional impact it is sometimes better to leave discussion until the following day, although in one or two instances the meaning will have to be elucidated. Each story should be read at one sitting, and where discussion is not required, as with *Grumphie*, timed to coincide with the end of the lesson. A page takes about 2–2½ minutes to read aloud.

Written Work

Pupils should not be asked to write slavish summaries of the stories, nor to perform a critical autopsy on each. A better method is to ask for the *occasional* résumé or imaginative story based on the pupil's own experience. It is also preferable at this level to omit any discussion of form or technique, but to regard the story primarily as a vehicle of meaning with a bearing on life. This volume is intended for use with *Excellence in English* Book 1 (Hodder and Stoughton) and follow-up exercises can be found there.

Acknowledgments

The author and publishers would like to thank the following for kindly granting permission for the reuse of copyright material in this book: Curtis Brown Ltd for 'Lost and Found' from *The Silver Trumpet* by Stuart Cloete and for 'A Message from the Pig-man' from *Nuncle* by John Wain; Barrie and Jenkins and J B S Haldane for 'Rats' from *My Friend Mr Leakey*; Rupert Crew Ltd for 'Grumphie' from *Kallee and Other Stories* by F G Turnbull; Hamish Hamilton Ltd for 'The Night the Ghost Got In' from *The Thurber Carnival* and 'Mr Monroe Outwits a Bat' from *The Owl in the Attic*, The Collection Copyright © 1963 Hamish Hamilton London; also Mrs Helen Thurber for 'The Night the Ghost Got In' copyright © 1933, 1961 James Thurber, from *My Life and Hard Times*, published by Harper & Row (originally printed in *The New Yorker*) and 'Mr Monroe Outwits a Bat' copyright © 1931, 1959 James Thurber, from *The Owl in the Attic* published by Harper & Row (originally printed in *The New Yorker*); Bill Naughton and George G Harrap and Co. Ltd for 'Spit Nolan' and 'The Goalkeeper's Revenge' from *The Goalkeeper's Revenge*; Dr Alan Paton and David Philip, Publisher (Pty) Ltd, Cape Town for 'The Quarry'; William Saroyan and Laurence Pollinger Ltd for 'The Parsley Garden' from *The Assyrian and Other Stories*; Emma Langland and Ward Lock Educational Ltd for 'Jenny' from *The Story-Teller*. Permission to reprint 'The Boy and the Badger' by E T Seton was granted by Anthony Sheil Associates Ltd; 'Luke Baldwin's Vow' by Morley Callaghan is reprinted by permission of A D Peters & Co Ltd; 'The Fun They Had', copyright © 1957 by Isaac Asimov from the book, *Earth is Room Enough* by Isaac Asimov: used by permission of Doubleday & Company Inc. and NEA, Services, Inc.